Out the Other Side

Sherryl D. Hancock

Published by Vulpine Press in the United Kingdom in 2020

ISBN: 978-1-83919-346-0

Cover by Claire Wood
Cover photo: Tirzah D. Hancock

www.vulpine-press.com

To all the fans of WeHo who have loved all of my girls, and followed them religiously, thank you! Sadly, this is the last planned full-length WeHo book; there will be no more new WeHo characters. But don't despair! You'll see the WeHo girls in special editions, and they may crop up in other series as well! Don't forget to look for the new Cal Fire – Smolder Series and the Castro Series coming soon!!! Much love and thanks to all of you!!!

Also in the WeHo series:

When Love Wins
When Angels Fall
Break in the Storm
Turning Tables
Marking Time
Jet Blue
Water Under the Bridge
Vendetta
Gray Skies
Everything to Everyone
Lightning Strykes
In Plain Sight
Quid Pro Qup
For the Telling
Between Heaven and Hell
Taking Chances
Darkness Past
Stonewall Pride (special anniversary edition)
When All Else Fails

Prologue

"You've got to be the coolest deputy director on the planet!" *Sydney Carson exclaimed as Harley pushed her Stillen Supercharged 370Z to its limits.*

On the radio blared M.I.A's "Bad Girls." The line about bad girls living fast fit the moment pretty well.

Harley grinned, enjoying the feeling of freedom her car's power always gave her.

Yes, she was the deputy director and chief information officer for the Governor's Office of Emergency Services. That was about as official as she ever got, with her longish white-blond hair and bright rainbow under-dye, which she usually wore in two long braids that extended three inches past the bottom of her hair so it was always on display. She was also the consummate tomboy, in her skinny jeans rolled up to expose her Harley-Davidson boots, her bright blue tank top with the words "Music On, World Off" in white print, and a denim jacket with a black hoodie liner. In her ears she had four silver hoops in graduated sizes, and in the bottom hole hung a chain with a small rainbow feather dangling from it.

Harley Marie Davidson didn't look like any regular executive.

"So, I'm thinkin'…" *Harley slowed her vehicle, knowing she was pushing her luck with California Highway Patrol and the Los Angeles Police Department. Sure, they knew her, but she wasn't sure they wouldn't call her boss, Gage McGinnis, to complain about her high-speed antics.*

1

"Okay…" Sydney said.

Sydney Carson was a twenty-three-year-old wunderkind in the computer world. In her dual-depth master's degree in computer science from Stanford University, she'd specialized in not only software theory but also systems. She could write programs and develop systems, and she could speak to people like Harley Davidson.

Harley had been writing computer programs for years. With a doctorate from MIT and experience with every level of law enforcement, both federal and state, she'd been an easy choice for CIO at OES. Gage McGinnis, having come from law enforcement, had seen in Harley a person she could work with, someone who understood the intricacies of, and the necessity of top security for, OES's programs in emergency situations.

Sydney and Harley had become fast friends. In Sydney, Harley had found a kindred spirit, in terms of programming, but also in their love of fast cars, and in a combination of mischief and an innate introversion that lent itself to shyness.

"What were you thinking?" Sydney prompted when Harley didn't continue.

Sydney knew her boss had ADHD and sometimes lost her train of thought, so prompting her was sometimes imperative; she'd learned that fairly quickly from Shiloh, Harley's assistant and girlfriend.

"Oh, sorry," Harley said, her mind having run off on her for a moment. "What classification are you right now?"

"I'm a senior IT analyst," Sydney said, looking confused. "Why?"

"Well, I'm thinking about making you a program manager."

Sydney stared back at Harley, shocked. "Uh, that's a huge jump."

"Yeah, I know, but I need someone that can get these guys out of the silo mentality in the programmer's unit, and I think that's you."

"And you don't think Anderson can do that?" Sydney asked.

"I think Anderson's an idiot," Harley said.

Sydney smiled; Harley always said what she thought, and she didn't pull any punches.

"Okay, but how's that going to track?" Sydney asked. "I mean with the other team members?"

"They like you, Syd," Harley said, "and they respect you, which is more than I can say for how they feel about Anderson."

"Yeah, but I'm only twenty-three, Harley. How are people going to feel about that?"

"I'm thirty-five," Harley said, shaking her head. "You think they don't all hate me for making deputy director?" She gave Syd a pointed look as she held up one rainbow braid. "Crazy shit and all? The thing is, I don't care what they think. I just need them to start working with me and not just for themselves."

Sydney knew what Harley meant. Everyone in the programming unit did their own thing; there was no team atmosphere. Harley had told her over and over again that they needed to be double-checking each other's work to try and identify issues in code long before they got to the demo stage. It was a source of embarrassment that quite often when their unit went to demonstrate a program they'd developed, it didn't work. Sydney completely agreed with Harley, but Anderson seemed to be more interested in fostering division among the programmers. Harley was fed up with it.

"So if I can do it, will you take the job?" Harley asked.

Sydney looked back at Harley, then finally shrugged. "I'm not stupid. That'd be a huge jump in pay for me—maybe I could finally move out of my parents' house and catch up on my mountain of student loan debt," she said with a grin.

"Okay, good."

Harley's phone rang; she hit the hands-free on the steering wheel. "'Lo?"

"Bangarang!" the woman on the other end of the line called.

"Bangarang!" Harley replied. "Hey, Jet, what's up?"

"Planning a run for this weekend. You in?" Jet asked.

"Bikes or cars?"

"Cars."

"Girls or no girls?" Harley asked then.

"No girls," Jet said, her grin on the other end of the line evident.

"Is Fadi ever going to get tired of being left behind?" Harley asked.

"Which is code for 'Shy's getting sick of it,'" Jet said. "We'll include the girls on the next one."

"Yeah, yeah, I'll tell Shy that," Harley said, shaking her head. "Yeah, I'm in. We doing it Saturday?"

"Yeah," Jet said. "Gonna rain again Sunday."

"So sick of this rain."

"Me too, but spring is right around the corner. You and Shy gonna be at the Club Friday?"

"Yeah," Harley said. "As long as I can get out of the damned office at some point."

"Rough being a boss, huh?" Jet asked, sounding far from sympathetic.

"Bite me, Jet," Harley said, grinning.

Jet chuckled. "We'll handle the details Friday then."

"Okay, later," Harley said, hanging up a moment later.

"Bangarang?" Sydney asked.

"Yeah," Harley said. "There's a group of us bois that hang out; we call ourselves the Lost Bois."

"But b-o-i-s, right?" Sydney asked, used to the term used for the butch lesbians.

"Right," Harley said. "Hey, you want to come on the run this weekend?"

"Would that be okay?"

"Sure," Harley said. "You'd fit in just fine. You're right about the same age as most of them. I'm actually one of the oldest."

Sydney looked at Harley, surprised; Harley never seemed very old to her.

"Yeah, I'd like to go," Sydney said. "Can I ride with you? My car isn't really up to a car like this."

Harley grinned. "Trust me, you ain't seen nothing," she said. "We got two classic Ferraris, a Porsche GTR, a Lambo, another 370Z but a Nismo, and depending on which one Jet brings, either a Maserati or a '67 Mustang Fastback."

"Whoa," Sydney said. "Yeah, I'm definitely not on par with any of that."

"Give the Lost Bois time, they'll get ya there," Harley said, grinning.

Sydney chuckled.

***

Gage McGinnis stirred, opening her eyes and turning her head. Her girlfriend, Kit, was lying next to her, leaning on her elbow, with her phone in her hand.

"Please don't tell me that on the first day off I've had in months, there's an emergency brewing," Gage said, her voice a groan.

Kit chuckled, her blue eyes twinkling. "No, I thought I'd try to go look at some apartments today."

Gage's brow furrowed. "What? Why?"

Kit's eyes searched Gage's. "I just... I mean, with Jack being convicted, I just thought that it would be time for Caitlyn and me to get out from underfoot..."

"You're not underfoot, Kit," Gage said. "I want you here. Don't you want to be with me anymore?" she asked, sounding concerned.

"I love being with you." Kit bit her lip. "But I just figure you probably need your space, and I don't want you to feel like you have to keep taking care of us."

Gage sat up, looking down at Kit. "Kit, I don't feel like I'm taking care of you," she said, her tone patient, but her expression indicating frustration. "I thought we were having a relationship... Am I wrong?"

"No," Kit said, sitting up at as well.

She looked up at the woman that was not only her girlfriend, lover, and boss, but also the woman who'd literally saved her life when her husband had tried to kill her. Gage McGinnis was, to Kit's way of thinking, a beautiful red-haired Irish warrior with fiery green eyes. The woman was exciting in ways Kit had never imagined, and Kit felt very lucky to be dating her. The night Gage had rescued her at gunpoint from Jack, she'd brought Kit back to the house she was staying in at the time. Kit and her four-year-old daughter, Caitlyn, had been staying there for the last three months, and Kit couldn't help but feel that she was a freeloader and that it would ruin her relationship with Gage. It was for that reason that she wanted to move, so that she and Gage could actually date without Gage having to deal with a four-year-old underfoot all the time and climbing into bed with them, which Caitlyn did often.

"I thought you might want to, like, actually date me instead of this sudden domesticity," Kit said. "You know, like normal relationships start and all."

Gage blinked, looking like she was reconciling what Kit was saying.

"Are you saying that's what you want?" Gage asked. "That you don't like things the way they are?"

"No, that's not what I'm saying," Kit said, not wanting Gage to think that she wasn't grateful for everything she'd done. "I just thought you might want your life back."

Gage stared back at Kit. "You and Caitlyn are my life," she said. "I mean, besides this ridiculous agency we're running," she added with a grin.

"I…" Kit stammered, looking stunned.

"Kit, I love you."

"You what?" Kit breathed, sure she hadn't heard Gage right, since there was this sudden roaring in her ears that was telling her she was an idiot.

Gage reached up and touched Kit's cheek, then leaned down to kiss her. "I love you."

"Oh," Kit said, sounding astounded. "I… I didn't know…"

"I know," Gage said, nodding. "I didn't say it because… well, I didn't want to freak you out."

"I think I've loved you since that first morning I met you," Kit said, shaking her head in wonder.

Gage beamed. "Love me, huh?"

"Yeah," Kit said, biting her lip.

"So don't go anywhere," Gage said. "I get that we didn't start out the standard way." Her eyes sparkled humorously. "Then again, we are lesbians. Moving at the speed of light is kind of our way."

Across town, Kashena Windwalker-Marshal woke to her partner on her phone. Turning over, she glanced up at her wife.

"Seriously?" Kashena asked.

Sierra trained dark eyes on her wife and saw a grin spread across Kashena's lips. She shook her head, her dark hair falling around her shoulders as her eyes flashed with subdued malice.

"I absolutely hate this new AG. She's completely different from Midnight."

"And obviously doesn't get the concept of Saturday morning," Kashena said, taking the phone out of Sierra's hand and tossing it to the end of the bed, then taking her wife in her arms, kissing her breathless.

Sierra stared up at Kashena, smiling. "I love you."

"I love you," Kashena replied, leaning down to kiss Sierra again. "And you know Gage is looking for a chief counsel for OES…"

"She is?" Sierra asked.

"Uh-huh," Kashena said, her expression becoming mischievous. "I could put in a good word for you… but you'd need to do something for me first." Her deep blue eyes widened.

Sierra narrowed her dark eyes at her wife. "That's called quid pro quo, Kashena Windwalker-Marshal, and it's illegal."

Kashena laughed. "Always the lawyer. I'm just trying to get laid here…" she said, her voice trailing off as she lowered her head to kiss Sierra's bare shoulder, then moved lower, taking a quickly hard nipple into her mouth.

"Oh," Sierra moaned softly, her hands immediately in Kashena's hair. "I guess if you really feel like you need… oh…"

They were making love moments later, and afterwards they lay together, both of them smiling as they tried to catch their breath.

"Seriously though, babe, Gage did ask me if I thought you would consider it, but that was before you really started to hate the new AG," Kashena told Sierra.

"Well, now I will definitely go and talk to her." Sierra glanced at her phone still lying at the end of the bed.

"Good," Kashena said, grinning.

***

Jocelyn returned from the bathroom, having thrown up again. She knew better than to drink coffee these days, but she did it anyway. She walked over to her desk. Pulling out her cigarettes and pocketing her lighter, she grabbed her jacket and walked outside.

Standing with her back to the building, she smoked, watching remotely as Gage's black Escalade drove into the parking lot. She knew she was avoiding Gage, but the fact was she knew that Gage didn't approve of what she was doing. If Jocelyn was honest with herself, she also knew it wasn't something she should be proud of; she was basically whoring her way around West Hollywood, sleeping with random women and dragging herself into the house in the wee hours of the morning. The few times she'd encountered Gage, she'd seen the disapproval in her friend's eyes and it had pissed her off. She'd managed to avoid a fight, literally biting her tongue and walking out of the room. She knew it was coming, though, and she was avoiding it for as long as possible.

Gage saw her standing at the side of the building. She leaned in and said something to Kit, and then walked her way as Kit went inside.

Jocelyn took a long drag on her cigarette, trying to draw as much nicotine into her system as she could before Gage reached her.

"Hey," Gage said as she walked up, taking out her own cigarette.

Jocelyn pulled her lighter out and lit Gage's cigarette. She knew that Gage was stressing, because she didn't smoke very often.

"What's going on?" Jocelyn asked, her usual protectiveness kicking in.

Gage looked surprised by the question. "I can't smoke with my best friend?"

Jocelyn gave her a knowing look. "In other words, I'm the stress that's causing you to smoke."

Gage considered her for a moment, debating trying to lie. Finally she blew her breath out and nodded. "You're scaring me, Gun."

"I'm just having a good time, Jock," Jocelyn said, shaking her head.

"You're out all hours of the night, Gun, and not just on the weekends anymore. You look like shit; you're running yourself into the ground."

"All of that?" Jocelyn asked in a wry tone, her eyes widening dramatically.

"You're killing yourself," Gage said seriously.

"I'm not," Jocelyn said, her voice sharper than she meant it to be. "I'm fine."

Gage narrowed her green eyes at her best friend. "I've known you for twenty years, Jos. You're not fine. I just need you to tell me what I can do to help."

"There's nothing that needs doing, Jock," Jocelyn said. "I get that you're all happy and domestic with Kit, but stop expecting me to do the same. It's not my thing. Our kid is having a kid of his own now, so it's time for me to cut loose, and that's what I'm doing, okay?"

Gage didn't believe her, not for a second, but she also knew that if she pushed too hard, Jocelyn would push back, and that wouldn't be a good thing. They'd had some knock-down drag-out fights before, and it was always bad, and it took a while to get over it. Gage had made Jocelyn her chief deputy director and couldn't afford a huge fight with her at this point. So she let it go for the time being.

"Are you losing weight?" Gage asked, canting her head to the side.

Jocelyn's lips twitched. "My stomach has been bothering me lately," she said. "Probably some flu or something."

Gage nodded, thinking she needed to try to keep better tabs on Jocelyn.

***

Shenin Hancock woke to the feeling of a hand on her stomach. She smiled as she felt Tyler's hand slide over her swollen belly and felt the baby move in response.

"He's responding to you," Shenin said, smiling up at her wife.

"You think so?" Tyler asked, her blue eyes looking thrilled with the prospect.

"Feel how he's moving? He's moving where your hand is." Shenin put her hand over Tyler's and moved it, feeling the baby move at the same time.

Tyler smiled brightly. "I think you're right," she said, moving her hand and kissing Shenin's belly softly.

Shenin put her hands in Tyler's long dark blond hair fondly, smiling down at her wife.

"We still need to come up with a name for him, you know," Shenin said.

Tyler nodded. "I know."

"Have you decided if you want to name him after your dad?"

"I don't think I want to saddle him with a 'junior' thing."

"Okay, then what boy names do you like? It has to roll off the tongue, you know," Shenin said, grinning.

"So you can yell at him like you do me? Using the whole name?" Tyler asked.

Shenin winked. "You got it."

"I've always liked the name Wheeler, but not for a first name," Tyler said. "Maybe a middle name. I don't want people calling him like Wheeley or something." Tyler rolled her eyes. "I'd have to go kick asses at the elementary school."

Shenin laughed. "No, that would be bad."

"What about something from your side?"

"I hate my father…" Shenin said.

"What about something Irish?"

"Hmm…" Shenin murmured. "What about Aiden?"

"Aiden Wheeler Hancock," Tyler said.

"Rolls off the tongue," Shenin said with a grin.

Tyler nodded. "Yes, it does."

"I like it."

"Then I'd say we have a baby name."

"I'd say so."

Chapter 1

"Uh, Gage," Shenin said hesitantly. "I think my water just broke... Oh!" The last was a loud gasp as a contraction ripped through her middle.

Gage stood up and moved around the conference room table to help Shenin up.

"Kit, call 911," she said calmly. "And get Gun in here."

"Okay," Kit said, responding to the calm in Gage's voice.

Twenty minutes later, people were gathered outside the conference room. There was no sign of the paramedics, and Shenin was in full labor. Sebastian had been called to pick her up and put her on the conference table; no one was taking any chances with Shenin at this point. Gage and Jocelyn were checking her, and Kit was doing her best to keep Shenin calm. Tyler had been called. Harley was busily working on hacking the local 911 dispatch to figure out where the ambulance was, with Shiloh standing by with her phone in case she needed to help Harley.

Sebastian walked into the conference room.

"Do you need me at all? You know, I've delivered three babies, two in a squad car."

"Not... unless... you can do it... with your eyes closed!" Shenin gritted out.

Sebastian laughed. "I think I'll go watch for Ty and the ambulance."

"Kit, can you see if anyone can locate some clean towels, and we need a blanket in case the baby comes."

"Okay, got it," Kit said, her eyes connecting with Gage's, looking worried.

Gage moved to Kit and hugged her gently. "She'll be okay, Kit, don't worry. We just need to stay calm to keep her calm," she whispered.

Kit nodded, letting her breath out slowly. Then she walked out of the conference room to talk to people about what was needed.

Tyler arrived a couple of minutes later, looking completely stressed.

"You got here fast," Gage said.

"Brought the bike, easier to move around traffic," Tyler said, moving to her wife. "So you thought you'd do this in dramatic style, huh?" she said softly, and she leaned down to kiss her.

"You... know... me," Shenin said, her voice halting with the pain she was in.

Tyler stood next to her, taking her hand. "I got you, babe. Just hold my hand." She looked worriedly at Gage and Jocelyn. "Where's the ambulance?"

"We've called," Gage said.

"Twice," Jocelyn added. "We may have to do this right here."

Tyler grimaced. It was far from optimal, and this was Shenin's first baby and a somewhat high-risk pregnancy due to scarring. She knew she needed to remain calm; if she freaked out, Shenin would too.

"I'm still trying to get somewhere with this damned system. It should be easier..." Harley said, her brain already thinking that she needed to create a system that would allow for this kind of calamity.

"Focus," Shiloh whispered to Harley.

Harley nodded, going back to it.

Kit returned with towels, blankets, and even a pillow that some-one had had in their car. They put the pillow under Shenin's head and covered her with a blanket, as well as putting one under her. Thankfully she was wearing a dress, so it was easy enough to remove her underwear to check the status of the baby.

Sebastian walked in again, staying at the other end of the confer-ence room table.

"I offered to help, but for some reason I was told no," he said, grinning.

"Yeah, you'd help over my dead body," Tyler said, giving him a narrowed look, even as a smirk curled her lips. She knew he was help-ing to keep everyone calm, and she appreciated it. She moved back to her wife, sliding her hand under Shenin and rubbing the small of her back.

"How you doing, honey?" she asked, her lips next to Shenin's ear.

"I'm scared, Ty…" Shenin whispered.

"It's going to be okay, baby. I'm right here, and I'm not going to let anything happen to you," Tyler said, tamping down firmly on her own fears.

"She's almost to ten," Jocelyn said, glancing over at Gage.

Gage nodded. "We're probably going to deliver this baby our-selves," she told Tyler. "Are you okay with Jos and I doing it? We've both done it before, once in Afghanistan, actually," she said, winking at Jocelyn.

Tyler swallowed convulsively. "I trust you," she said, her blue eyes reflecting her fear for her wife.

Gage looked over at Jocelyn, and Jocelyn nodded. Without a word they both went to the antibacterial solution located in the conference

15

room for cold and flu season. They used the solution and dried their hands.

"Never thought I'd be doing this again," Jocelyn murmured to Gage.

"Me either," Gage said, "but we are the Office of Emergency Services, right?"

"Yeah, you'd think the fucking fire department could find us," Jocelyn said with a grin.

With that, they went back to Shenin. Jocelyn checked Shenin again.

"Okay, Shen, you're fully dilated. You need to start pushing," Jocelyn said.

Gage moved to Shenin's other side, taking her other hand. "Okay, when you feel a contraction start, you need to bear down as hard as you can, and we're going to count to ten. Then you can relax till the next one, alright?"

Shenin looked up at Gage, seeing how calm she was, and nodded before glancing at Tyler again. The next contraction came, and Shenin strained and cried out.

"Ty," Gage said, "get up on the table behind her, holding her up. Kash, can you come take Ty's place?"

Kashena took Tyler's place as Tyler pulled off her riding jacket and sat behind her wife, taking the upper half of Shenin's body and leaning it against her chest. They went through the next few contractions, and it was obvious that Shenin was having a rough time.

"Okay, let's try this," Gage said. "Shenin, turn on your side. That's how I ended up delivering Mark; for some reason it was easier."

Shenin nodded, and Kashena helped her move to her side; Sebastian stepped in, helping her turn. He then moved to the end of the table, putting his back to Tyler's to support her so she could better hold Shenin.

Kit watched her girlfriend and her friends work together to help Shenin, and she felt a huge swell of pride. Looking around at the faces of the people outside the conference room, she could see that they were all completely entranced with these people. They were watching the deputy directors work together to help each other, and it said a lot about who they were.

"They're stuck in traffic," Harley muttered. "There's a pile-up."

Gage glanced over at Jocelyn. "Okay, Shen, it's just us now. We can do this. I promise you that you can do this."

Shenin nodded, blowing her breath out and looking up at Tyler.

"I'm right here, babe," Tyler said. "We can do this."

Shenin nodded again, seeming as if she were drawing strength directly from Tyler's words.

There was another twenty minutes of pushing and breathing, and a few more outcries, but finally Aiden Wheeler Hancock made his appearance in the world. Jocelyn delivered him and immediately cleared his mouth and nose, and he issued a fairly annoyed cry, causing his mothers to laugh.

"Don't smack me, Ty," Jocelyn said as she dried Aiden off, "but, Shenin, unbutton the top of that dress." She gave a wicked grin.

"Hey…" Tyler said as she assisted Shenin.

Jocelyn laid Aiden on Shenin's chest. "It's best if you can get him to nurse," she said, putting a blanket over both Shenin and the baby.

Shenin smiled up at Tyler. Tyler kissed her.

"You did it, babe," she said softly, her eyes shining with unshed tears.

Shenin reached for Tyler's hand. "We did it."

"Let's give these three some privacy." Gage nodded toward the door to the conference room.

"Thank you," Tyler said, looking at Gage and Jocelyn, and then at Sebastian, Kashena, Kit, Harley and Shiloh. "All of you."

"That's what we do." Kashena smiled at Tyler, leaning in to kiss the other woman on the temple and putting her hand to Shenin's cheek.

"Well, that was fun," Jocelyn said as they walked out of the conference room to a round of applause from the staff.

"And that," Gage said to the staff, "is how you handle an emergency," she said, smiling and receiving a lot of laughs for it.

"The ambulance is here!" someone called.

"Not a moment too soon," Jocelyn said, rolling her eyes.

"Baz, can you go lead them in?" Gage asked.

"You got it," Sebastian said.

Gage stuck her head back into the conference room. "Ty, the ambulance is here. I want them to take you two to the hospital to make sure Shen and the baby are okay. Alright?"

"Yeah," Tyler said, nodding.

Kimber found Jocelyn at the side of the building, smoking, a half an hour later.

"Wow, that was dramatic," Kimber said.

Jocelyn shrugged. "It is what it is."

"You were pretty great in there though," Kimber said, touching Jocelyn's jawline.

Jocelyn's eyes went to Kimber's, and she raised an eyebrow at the girl.

"What?" Kimber asked.

Jocelyn simply shook her head, looking away and continuing to smoke.

"So, would you come over later?" Kimber asked.

"Why?"

Kimber gaped at her openmouthed, then shrugged, trying to appear unconcerned. "You just haven't been over in a while."

"Because you got all friggin' weirded out last time," Jocelyn said.

"I said I was sorry about that."

"Yeah, and that's fine," Jocelyn said, "but I don't think it's a good idea that we hang out anymore."

"Why?" Kimber asked in a near-whine. "I miss you..."

Jocelyn looked back at her in disbelief.

Kimber pressed against Jocelyn. "Come over tonight. I promise to make it worth your time..."

Jocelyn narrowed her eyes, stepping away from Kimber.

"Please?" Kimber begged.

Jocelyn finally sighed. "Okay, fine, I'll come by."

"Great!" Kimber said, smiling.

That night, Jocelyn arrived at Kimber's apartment, and Kimber greeted her completely naked. Jocelyn walked inside, kicking the door closed, and picked the girl up, carrying her into her bedroom, where she laid her down. Kimber pulled Jocelyn down on the bed and began kissing her, her hands pulling at Jocelyn's jacket. Jocelyn stood up, shrugged out of her jacket and kicked off her boots.

They were in the middle of having sex when Jocelyn suddenly felt her stomach lurch. She jumped up and ran to the bathroom to throw up. She noted a little bit of blood, and her lips twitched; she wondered if that was just part of it, or if this was a whole new thing. Sitting on the floor of the bathroom, she waited for the nausea to pass. That was when the fatigue took over. It took all of her strength to pull herself up off the floor. She walked back into the room and lay down on the bed. Kimber was watching her.

"Are you okay?" she asked.

"Just need to rest," Jocelyn muttered, lying down on her stomach.

Kimber got up and paced for a few minutes. Finally she put her bathrobe on and left the room. Jocelyn slept for an hour, and then dragged herself out of Kimber's bed and got dressed. When she walked out into the living room, Kimber looked up from her iPad.

"Where are you going?" she asked.

"Home," Jocelyn said, feeling her stomach lurch again.

"But..." Kimber started to say something, but Jocelyn's raised eyebrow stopped her.

Kimber simply nodded. Jocelyn walked out of the apartment and got down to the Viper. It took all her strength to drive back to Lenna's house, but she made it. Fortunately, it wasn't a long drive.

Once at the house, she dragged herself inside, going straight into her room and dropping on her bed. She fell asleep with all her clothes and even her boots on. It was the first thing Gage saw the next morning when she checked on her.

Gage was still shaking her head when she walked back into the bedroom she and Kit were in.

"She's off the rails," Gage said in a low voice.

"Is she home?" Kit asked, knowing Gage was worried about Jocelyn.

"Yeah, but it looks like she passed out in her clothes. She didn't even take off her boots."

Kit grimaced, understanding what Gage meant.

"I've never seen her like this," Gage said, "and I can't stand by and let her kill herself..."

"What can we do?" Kit asked.

Gage looked contemplative, then she picked up her phone. She pulled up her contacts and hit a number. She put the phone to her ear, her eyes connecting with Kit's as she waited for the person to answer. Kit could only hear Gage's side of the conversation, but she could easily figure out who Gage was talking to.

"Hi, it's Gage... I'm good. Look, I'm calling you about Gun... Well, she's shit right now, that's the thing... She's completely off the rails and I can't get through to her... She's basically killing herself slowly... I don't know what happened between you two that had you running scared, but if you care about her at all, you'll get back here and at least talk to her about it... Because I'm afraid I'm going to be burying my best friend in the next few months, that's why," she said in almost a growl.

Apparently that hit home with Sable, because Gage let her breath out in a relieved sigh. She hung up a few minutes later.

"She's coming," Gage said, setting her phone down.

"You think it's the breakup with Sable that's sent her spinning?" Kit asked.

"Yeah," Gage said. "I know Jos. She's been a slut before, but not like this, and not to the point of it affecting her work or endangering her own life or others'. If she's driving after she ties one on and is so out of it she passes out fully clothed... she's out of control."

"And it all started after Sable left."

"Exactly," Gage said. "So if there's even a remote chance that's what it is, then I need Sable's ass back here to fix it."

Kit suppressed a grin. Sable was a worldwide-known rock star, and Gage was talking about her like any other person. Then again, Gage had grown up with a mother who was a world-renowned rock star, so rock stars didn't really intimidate her much.

21

"Are you kidding me?" Shiloh asked when she turned over on Saturday morning and Harley was already awake and texting.

Harley's blue eyes shifted to her, and Shiloh could read confusion in them.

"Who are you texting at..." Shiloh glanced at the clock on the nightstand. "Five thirty on a Saturday?"

"Syd," Harley said.

"Aren't you going to see her in like three and a half hours?"

"Yeah," Harley said, "but I may have forgotten the fix I have for this particular bug in the program by then..." Her voice trailed off as she tapped out another message.

"Can't you just send yourself a message with the fix?" Shiloh asked, becoming annoyed.

"I could, but—" Harley began to say, but then her phone pinged and she started to look at the message.

Shiloh sat up and plucked the phone from Harley's hand, tossing it aside. Harley's mouth opened to protest, but Shiloh pressed her nude body against Harley's, her lips going to Harley's neck, the one thing she knew Harley couldn't ignore.

"I... oh..." Harley began, ending on a low moan. "Shy..." she groaned moments later, her hands sliding up Shiloh's back, one hand making its way into Shiloh's hair to hold the back of her head right where it was.

Shiloh continued to kiss Harley's neck, making a point of sucking at her skin, hard enough to leave a mark. Harley's hands grasped at her as she breathed heavily.

"Shy, Shy…" she chanted, shifting to put Shiloh under her and pressing her body over her, moving rhythmically.

Shiloh pulled Harley closer and pressed her body upward. They came together, exclaiming out loud. Afterwards, Harley moved to Shiloh's side, her hand still on Shiloh's stomach, her other arm under Shiloh's neck, holding her close.

Shiloh rested her head against Harley's shoulder. "I love you," she said, touching the long rainbow braid that hung down.

Harley smiled, her blue eyes searching Shiloh's. "I love you too, Shy."

Shiloh snuggled against Harley, just wanting to keep her this close. But before long the pinging of Harley's phone distracted her. Shiloh could feel Harley practically vibrating under her head. Finally, sighing, Shiloh sat up, picked up Harley's phone, and handed it to her.

"ADHD is a bitch," Harley said, grinning.

"I know. I hate that bitch sometimes," Shiloh said seriously as she got up to go and make coffee, knowing that was the next thing Harley would need.

She also knew it would only be a matter of time before Sydney arrived at the house for their latest Lost Bois run. And since it would be the first time Sydney had been at their place, there was likely to be a tour of the expansive house and she'd get no time with Harley after that. She was doing her best to be supportive of Harley's participation in the bois' group, because she knew that they were helping Harley become less focused on work. It had become more difficult when Sydney had joined the group.

Sydney Carson worked directly with Harley on a regular basis. She was a fellow programmer and while completely sweet and seemingly harmless, she was also quite hot in a cute, baby-butch kind of way. Shiloh couldn't help but wonder if there was more going on between Harley and Sydney. They were together all the time, and it was obvious Sydney had a serious hero-worship thing going on for Harley. Shiloh just wasn't sure if the hero-worship had or would turn into a crush and then more. Harley wasn't very good at detecting when someone was into her. There'd been any number of times in the nearly three years they'd been dating that some woman at the Club or at DOJ, where they'd previously worked, had made eyes at Harley and she hadn't even caught it. It usually took Shiloh pointing it out to Harley to make her see it, and even then, Harley was so blasé about it that it was impossible to get her to put the person off.

Such had been the case with Kimber Shell at OES. After a conversation where Kimber had made it quite clear to Harley that she wanted to sleep with her, and even Shiloh, Harley still hadn't been sure the girl hadn't been kidding. She'd told Shiloh about the conversation, and Shiloh had been the one to warn Kimber off, letting her know that Harley was very taken and that she better not mess with that. Kimber still made passes at Harley all the time, but Harley either simply ignored them, or she shook her head. Shiloh was ready to kill the little blonde.

If Sydney was after Harley, though, she was smarter than to be direct about it, and that was what worried Shiloh the most.

Two hours later, Harley was sitting out in the backyard, smoking, when the doorbell rang. Shiloh answered the door and scrutinized Sydney. At the age of twenty-three, Sydney had short dark-brown hair that stuck up at the front, with a few small sections that hung down on her forehead. She also sported small gauges in her ears; today's set was neochrome, which gave her an edgy look. She had a slim build that allowed her to wear pretty much anything. Today's outfit was a black tank top, white jeans worn low on her hips, showing black boxer briefs that said "Tomboy" on the rainbow waistband, and black-and-white Converse sneakers. She was the ultimate tomboy, with the young, edgy style that seemed to turn a lot of heads.

Sydney smiled bashfully at Shiloh, her gold-colored eyes sparkling in the morning sunlight.

"Good morning, Shiloh," Sydney said, always feeling really shy around Harley's beautiful girlfriend.

"Good morning, Syd." Shiloh, as always, felt bad about her ill feelings about Sydney when she smiled at her like that. "Come on in," she said, opening the door wider. "Harley's in the backyard."

Sydney walked into the house, her jaw dropping at the huge, beautiful entryway.

"Holy cow..." she muttered.

"Yeah, I had the same reaction the first time Harley brought me here too," Shiloh said, smiling. "Do you want some coffee?"

Sydney shook her head, holding up the can of Rockstar in her hand.

"Ugh, I don't know how you drink that stuff first thing in the morning."

Sydney shrugged. "Been doing it for about ten years now, so..."

"Since you were thirteen?"

Sydney grinned impishly.

"Your parents should be shot," Shiloh muttered.

Sydney chuckled, spying Harley in the backyard and heading that way.

"This place is sick!" Sydney exclaimed as she walked out into the backyard.

Harley glanced up, looking around her. "Yeah, I like it."

"Never realized what a baller you really are." Sydney walked over and sat down next to Harley.

25

Shiloh stood inside, watching the two talking. She could see Harley talking excitedly and knew that it had to do with a computer program—that was the kind of thing Harley got excited about.

An hour later, Harley and Sydney were getting ready to leave. Harley walked over to stand behind Shiloh, who was sitting on the couch reading a book.

"Headed out, babe," Harley said, kissing Shiloh on the top of the head.

"Uh-uh," Shiloh uttered, pulling Harley back down to her. She leaned her head back, sliding her hands up into Harley's hair, grasping two handfuls and pulling her closer to kiss her deeply.

Sydney watched from the kitchen, her eyes widening.

In the car a minute later, Sydney looked over at Harley. "And how sprung are you right now after that kiss?"

Harley grinned, her blue eyes twinkling as she started her car. "She kinda likes me," she said wryly.

"Ya think?" Sydney queried.

Harley laughed, nodding her head.

"We seriously need to get that kid hooked up," Jet said to Skyler as they watched Sydney sitting with Cody, Dakota and Harley in another booth.

"I don't get it," Skyler said, shaking her head. "She's got the style. Why doesn't she use it?"

A cute girl had just walked by the table, giving all the bois the look. Sydney, the only one who was single and could do anything about that, had simply smiled shyly and gone back to talking to Harley.

The girl passed Jet and Skyler, who did make a rather enticing pair, with their light-colored eyes and dark hair. Jet had a tendency to flirt, but she also had a platinum wedding band firmly on her left hand that she tended to display as well. The girl winked at both Jet and Skyler and continued toward the bathroom.

"Bangarang," Jet said, grinning. "You know, in the old days I'd have followed her…" She shook her head wistfully.

"Uh-huh," Skyler said. "I'm with ya there, but I'll stick with my wife."

"Yeah, me too." Jet smiled, thinking of her young wife, who she'd gone all the way to Iraq to rescue from the clutches of ISIS.

"So what can we do to hook the kid up?" Skyler asked, going back to the original conversation.

"Her birthday is next month. We could start by taking her to a strip club. Maybe she can test out some skills there."

"Are you sure she has any?" Skyler asked.

"Well, she's got potential," Jet said.

Skyler looked back at Jet skeptically. "She's cute, but…" She shook her head.

"Syd!" Jet yelled.

Sydney turned her head. "What?"

Jet put her hand up, using her index finger to indicate to Sydney that she needed to stand. Sydney gave her an odd look but stood up, facing Jet. People in the restaurant glanced over, and Sydney pressed her lips together, already embarrassed.

"Shirt," Jet said with a mischievous look.

"What?" Sydney asked, her eyes wide.

"Lift it," Jet said, looking at Skyler pointedly.

Skyler shook her head but looked over at Sydney too, making the same kind of "up" gesture Jet had made. Sydney rolled her eyes at the ceiling but did as the other two bid and lifted up the bottom of her tank top, holding her other hand out plaintively. She was, however,

27

exposing a fairly nice expanse of tanned and toned abdominal muscles, and even the top of the V of her pelvic bone was sexily displayed.

"Oh," Skyler murmured. "I see your point."

The girl who'd walked by them earlier chose that moment to walk back toward her table, seeing what Sydney was doing. Sydney immediately dropped her shirt and her head at the same time in complete mortification.

"Nice," the girl said as she passed Sydney.

"Bangarang!" Jet and Skyler called together.

"Bangarang!" the rest of the group answered, except for Sydney, who was wishing she could hide under the table.

***

"You're Colby's mother?" the woman asked, looking at Kashena oddly.

"One of them," Kashena replied, her grin wry. "That's his other mother." She nodded to Sierra, who was walking toward them.

"I—oh," the woman stammered.

Kashena couldn't help the evil smile that crept across her face. Sierra saw it immediately and knew that Kashena was screwing with the straights again.

"You must be Mrs. Stanhope," Sierra said, extending her hand to the teacher.

"I, well, yes," Mrs. Stanhope said as she shook hands with Sierra, her eyes veering from Sierra to Kashena and then back again.

"Yes, we're gay," Kashena said, her blue eyes widening like it was a shocking statement. "And married and everything…"

"I, well, I understand," Mrs. Stanhope said, looking everywhere but at Kashena.

"You'll have to forgive my wife," Sierra said, narrowing her dark eyes at Kashena. "She's rather incensed about the recent attack on our son for having two lesbians for mothers."

The teacher nodded, looking at Kashena again and seeing the malicious glint in her eyes as her lips twitched.

"Mom!" Colby yelled as he ran over to the group, throwing himself into Kashena's arms.

"Heya, handsome!" Kashena said, smiling. "How was camp?"

"It was alright," Colby said, hugging Sierra and kissing her cheek.

"Uh," Kashena murmured as she touched the slight bruise on his cheek, "what's that about?"

"I was learning some taekwondo," Colby said.

Kashena grinned. "I see. Learning to defend yourself is smart."

"Especially if stupid people are going to continue to exist on this planet," Colby said, grinning back.

"Got that right." Kashena's eyes skipped over to the teacher, who still looked extremely uncomfortable. "Let's go," she said, nodding toward her car.

Colby started to head to the car. Kashena turned to the teacher again, extending her hand. "It's been a real pleasure," she said, her tone far from sincere.

The teacher took Kashena's hand and felt the strength there. Her eyes widened. Kashena only smiled.

"Had to screw with the teacher, right?" Sierra asked on the way home.

"I can guarantee you that she's the one that excused those boys' behavior," Kashena said.

"Maybe so, but you do remember innocent until proven guilty, right?" Sierra asked.

"That's lawyer stuff, babe. I'm a cop."

"Not anymore," Colby put in from the back seat.

"Don't make me come back there," Kashena said.

Colby only laughed, shaking his head.

When they got home, Kashena and Sierra went into the house. Colby followed, putting his camping gear away. An hour later, he found his mothers sitting in the living room, watching a movie. He stood looking at them.

Kashena was sitting with her back to the corner of the large sectional. Sierra sat next to her, her back against Kashena's side. Kashena's left arm was around Sierra, and Sierra's left hand was holding Kashena's, their fingers interlaced. Sierra's right arm rested on Kashena's legs, which were extended in front of her. They looked so comfortable together, and Colby was so happy to see it. A few years before, things were a mess, and they were fighting; then Kashena had almost been killed by Colby's father, an ex-Marine like Kashena, but one who hated her.

"What are you guys watching?" Colby asked as he walked into the room.

"*San Andreas*," Kashena said.

"Getting some tips?" Colby asked.

"Yeah," Kashena said, grinning. "On what not to do in an emergency."

Kashena was his stepmother, having married Sierra, his biological mother, but he loved Kashena just as much as he did Sierra. What's more, he respected Kashena a great deal—she was teaching him to be a good man, and he knew that his life was better for her being in it.

"Kash, can I borrow you for a sec?" Colby asked, tugging at his bottom lip, something Kashena knew he did when he was nervous.

"Sure," Kashena said, kissing Sierra as she got up off the couch.

Kashena picked up her jacket and pulled it on as they walked out to the back patio. Kashena proceeded to light a cigarette, sitting down and looking over at Colby.

"What's up, Col?"

Colby sat down, seeing how confident Kashena looked, her sapphire-blue eyes gazing at him expectantly.

"I wanted to ask you a question," Colby said hesitantly.

"Okay, ask," Kashena said, smiling.

She could see that he was nervous, and she was definitely curious as to what this was about. With the incident at school a couple weeks back, it had come into specific relief that Colby was different from the other kids that went to his school. Most of the other kids at the charter school were upper class and came from standard rich family backgrounds. Not a two-lesbian household where one mother was a cop and the other a lawyer. It had also become widely known that Kashena had been attacked and almost killed by Sierra's ex-husband. Sierra had been worried that Colby would begin resenting them for being different. Kashena was wondering if this conversation had anything to do with that.

"Before you were with Mom, did you date a lot of women?" Colby asked, surprising Kashena completely.

"Uh... maybe. Why?"

"Maybe?" Colby gave her a deadpan look. "You know, I can ask Baz..."

"You stay away from Baz," Kashena said, scowling, but then began to smile. "Okay, yeah, I dated some. Why?"

"So you probably know how to flirt with girls, right?" Colby asked.

Kashena laughed at that. "Not that your mother knows of, no."

"Oh, I've heard Mom refer to you as a stud a few times; I think she probably knows," Colby said with a grin.

Kashena smiled, looking embarrassed as she scratched her head.

"So why do you need to know this?" Kashena asked, anxious to move the conversation away from her previous love life, which had indeed included a lot of women.

"Well, I met this girl at camp… and I don't know how to know if she likes me or not."

Kashena smiled widely, nodding slowly.

"I see," she said, "and you think I can help how?"

"Well, how do you know when a girl's interested in you?" Colby asked.

Kashena took a pause, taking a thoughtful draw off her cigarette and blowing the smoke out slowly.

"Tell me this—how'd you meet her?" she asked.

"She was working in the horse arena and couldn't pick something up. I saw her struggling with it and went and helped her."

Kashena smiled proudly. "That's my boy."

Colby smiled too, seeing the pride on Kashena's face and feeling a warm glow that his mother was proud of him. It had been Kashena's influence that had made him help the girl—she'd always told him that he didn't just want to be any man; he wanted to be a gentleman. She'd also told him that women were always to be treated with the utmost respect, unless they proved they didn't deserve it.

"So how did she react to you helping her?" Kashena asked.

"She smiled and said thank you," Colby said, "but then she didn't really talk to me after that. I didn't want to be a total dork, so I walked away."

"Do you think she's shy?"

Colby looked considering for a moment, then shrugged. "I don't know. I mean, she seemed to have a lot of friends…"

"That doesn't always mean a girl isn't shy, Col," Kashena said.

"Okay," Colby said. "So what should I do?"

"So have you seen her around school?"

"Well, I know some of the people she hangs out with, yeah."

"Okay, so when you get back to school, you make a point of wandering by wherever she and her friends hang out." Kashena marveled at the fact that she was telling her teenage son how to hit on girls. "Then when you get a chance, you just ask her how her day is going or if she likes her classes, or whatever, just something to get her to look at you and see that you're paying attention."

Colby pulled at his lower lip, nodding.

"Is she a girly girl or kind of a tomboy?" Kashena asked.

"What's the difference?"

Kashena laughed. "Okay, so your mom, she's a girly girl—makeup, hair, all that. Women like Devin or Natalia, they're girly girls. The tomboys are the ones like Skyler, or Memphis, or Cody and Dakota."

"Oh, she's definitely more like Mom and Natalia," Colby said with a shy smile.

Kashena grinned. She knew that Colby had a bit of a crush on Natalia because at their last party, Natalia had told him how handsome he was and ran her finger along his jawline. The poor kid looked like he was going to die. Admittedly, Natalia was a fairly hot Latina who could make a dead man or woman rise to the occasion.

"Okay, I can tell you that the girly girls really like for you to notice what they go through to look good for you… so if she's cool with you and talks to you a little bit, you could go so far as to compliment her. Just make sure it's not over the top."

"What do you mean, over the top?" Colby asked.

"Like, don't tell her she's the most beautiful girl you've ever met... at least not at first, okay?"

Colby grinned. "Have you told Mom that?"

"Repeatedly, but I know she likes me," Kashena said, laughing.

"Okay. What should I say, then?"

"Well, if she's wearing a shirt that looks good on her, you can say something like 'That looks really good on you,' or if she's got beautiful eyes, you can say something about that—just don't go for the whole 'limpid pools' or any of that crap. Keep it real. Something like 'You have the bluest eyes...' and let your voice trail off."

Colby nodded. "Okay, yeah, I get it."

"And what's going on out here?" Sierra asked, having gone into the kitchen to get a drink and heard Kashena's comment.

Kashena and Colby smiled at each other.

"Kash is teaching me how to flirt with girls," Colby said.

Sierra walked over, her dark eyes on her wife. "Well, she'd know how."

"What's that supposed to mean?" Kashena asked, grinning.

"It means I know damned good and well you were as bad as Baz was with the women in the old days, Kashena Windwalker-Marshal."

"You got no proof, counselor," Kashena said.

"That's what you're gonna go with, huh?" Sierra asked, her smile wide.

"Maybe?"

"I can worm a confession out of Baz with both hands tied behind my back, babe..."

"Damn," Kashena said, dropping her head.

"It's okay," Sierra said, sitting on the arm of Kashena's chair and taking her hand. "As long as I'm the only one you flirt with now, we're good."

"Well, that's no problem," Kashena said, smiling up at Sierra.

Chapter 2

"Goddamn it, Gun, don't make me fucking pit your car!" Gage yelled.

She was speeding after Jocelyn, who'd left the house in a blind rage. Gage had no idea what had pissed Jocelyn off; all she knew was that she had to stop her before she got into a heavy-traffic area. The Viper careened down the curved streets of the east hills, and Gage was struggling to catch up in the Escalade.

"Make sure your seatbelt is secure," Gage told Kit.

Kit looked worriedly over at Gage but did what she said, making sure her seatbelt was on tight.

Gage kept hitting the horn, trying to get Jocelyn's attention and influence her to slow down.

"I fuckin' hate that car right now," Gage muttered. "Too fucking fast, Gun. Too fast…"

Kit looked at her phone as it pinged; it was a text from Lenna.

"Gage, your mom says that Gun's been drinking," Kit said.

"Fuckin' A!" Gage raged. "Is she fucking trying to kill herself?"

They both grimaced as Jocelyn took a curve really fast and the back end of the Viper kicked out slightly. Jocelyn was able to correct the slide before she went over the edge of the road, but it was close. Many parts of the roads at this level were drop-offs, and if Jocelyn lost it on the wrong one…

"Damn it! Hold on!" Gage said, pushing the gas pedal of the Escalade down harder. The vehicle leaped forward.

Catching up to the Viper, Gage edged forward, moving to the side of Jocelyn's back end. She carefully edged over, lightly tapping the back fender of the Viper. It was a technique called a touch and go, and it was a prelude to a maneuver called a PIT maneuver. A precision immobilization technique would have Gage's vehicle tapping the back end of Jocelyn's car and forcing her to spin. It was a dangerous move to do on someone that was already in a shitty mood, and it would definitely take the chance of damaging both cars, and possibly crashing. Gage knew Jocelyn would know what she was warning her about, and she was hoping it would make Jocelyn give up rather than take the chance that Gage would do a PIT maneuver on her vehicle with the possibility it would get damaged in the process.

"Are you fucking kidding me!" Jocelyn yelled in her car. "Fucking PIT my car, see what I fucking do to ya!"

Shoving the clutch in, Jocelyn downshifted and jammed her foot down on the gas. The Viper leaped ahead. She continued along the road at top speed. She frankly didn't care if she ended up at the bottom of a cliff, but the last damned thing she wanted to do was to take Gage with her. She knew she needed to get away from her, and with that in mind, her driving became that of a precision race-car driver. Gage had no hope of keeping up at those speeds.

"Goddamn her!" Gage shouted, finally slowing and pulling over to the side of the road.

She knew she'd lost any hope of getting to Jocelyn. Instead she pulled out her phone and started making calls. She tapped every friend she had in Los Angeles with the PD, Sheriff's Department and Highway Patrol.

"Just keep an eye open for her, will ya?" Gage asked the fifth person she'd talked to by that time. "Thanks, I appreciate it."

37

Gage hung up her phone, pocketed it and put the Escalade in gear again, turning it around to head back up the hill.

"Are you okay?" Kit asked, knowing that Gage was worried.

"Where the fuck is Sable?" Gage asked, sounding annoyed. "She said she'd come, but that was a fucking week ago."

Kit bit her lip; she didn't know what to tell Gage. She knew that Gage was extremely worried about Jocelyn, and it was starting to take its toll on her. She almost never slept anymore, until she was completely exhausted. Kit did everything she could to help, but whereas Gage had been able to sleep with Kit, much as she had with Jocelyn, that no longer seemed to work. Kit knew that it was Gage's worry that was keeping her awake nights.

Jocelyn wouldn't talk to either of them, and she seemed to be getting worse and worse. When she was at the house, she stayed in her room and only came out to leave for work. Gage was fairly sure Jocelyn was no longer eating except what little it took to keep her alive. Jocelyn had lost a shocking amount of weight; even with her tall frame, it was very obvious.

And now she was drinking and then driving? It wasn't the Jocelyn that Gage knew, and it scared the hell out of her.

It was a long night, waiting to see if Jocelyn would come home or if they'd get a call that said she'd wrapped her car around a tree or lamppost. No call ever came, and Jocelyn never came home. Gage got reports from CHP that Jocelyn's Viper had been spotted doing one hundred and twenty on I-5 North toward Bakersfield.

Jocelyn didn't come back that weekend, but she must have dragged in at some point Sunday night because she was in the kitchen drinking coffee on Monday morning like nothing had happened.

"Think you should maybe eat something with that?" Gage asked in an acerbic tone.

"Think you should mind your own business?" Jocelyn replied, her tone equally barbed.

Gage's jaw twitched. The desire to smack her best friend was really strong at that moment. Kit touched her arm, shaking her head. The last thing they wanted was for Jocelyn to get so mad that she left Lenna's house completely; then they'd have no way to keep tabs on her.

Gage and Kit left the house a few minutes later. Jocelyn beat them to the office regardless and was in her office with her door closed when they arrived. Gage shook her head as she walked by Jocelyn's door.

Later that day, Jocelyn walked out to her car and noted someone sitting against the right fender. She scowled as she realized it was Sable. Her lips curled in derision as she opened the trunk to put her bag into it.

"What the hell are you doing here?" Jocelyn asked, her voice low.

"Here for a visit," Sable said brightly, her eyes far from convincing, however.

Jocelyn moved to the driver's side of the car, looking at Sable over the roof.

"Gage call you?" Jocelyn asked, her expression far from happy.

"She said you're off the rails," Sable said, looking worried.

Jocelyn gave a humorless laugh; even so, she hit the unlock button for the passenger side of the car and then got in on the driver's side. Without a word, Jocelyn started the engine. Sable hastily got into the car, worried that Jocelyn would drive off without her. In the car, music poured from the speakers. Breaking Benjamin's "Follow" was on.

Sable listened to the words as Jocelyn sang them, driving the Viper at breakneck speeds. Part of the song made Sable wonder if it was what Jocelyn was truly thinking. She wondered if Jocelyn really wanted to cut the strings that kept her safe. It was a disturbing thought.

Sable could see exactly why Gage was completely freaked out. Jocelyn looked gaunt and drawn, like she'd lost at least twenty pounds, maybe more. Her skin was pale; she wasn't the vibrant healthy woman she'd been six months before, and it was terrifying to see in person.

After forty-five minutes of music and no conversation, Jocelyn finally turned the stereo down, glancing over at Sable.

"So what do you want, Sable?" she asked, her tone flat.

Sable gave Jocelyn a measuring look. "Gage thinks that your spiral started when I left," she said evenly. "I want to know if that's true."

Jocelyn's face twisted into a sneer, and Sable expected her to deny it had anything to do with her.

"Yeah, that got the ball rolling." She shrugged, her eyes unreadable.

"I didn't think it would matter that much," Sable said honestly.

Jocelyn raised an eyebrow. "I guess I overestimated what I meant to you."

"And I thought it was me who had overestimated things," Sable countered.

"How so?" Jocelyn asked, mystified. "You're the one that fucking left."

"Because I had to," Sable said.

"Why?"

Sable gave Jocelyn a long, searching look. Finally she blew her breath out.

"You really don't know, do you?" Sable asked in surprise.

40

"I've absolutely no fucking clue," Jocelyn said.

"Remember the night that Gage texted you while we were at dinner? Telling you that she'd dislocated her shoulder?"

"Yeah…"

"And after you'd put it back into place and got her an icepack, she told you to go take care of your girl…" Sable said.

Jocelyn nodded, still looking completely lost.

"You said you were, and that you'd go take care of Sable 'now,'" Sable said, her gaze flickering in remembered pain at the thought.

"Okay…" Jocelyn said, her tone indicating she still had no idea what Sable was talking about.

"You basically said that she was your girl, and that I was… second in line."

Jocelyn's mouth dropped open, then she closed it, blinking slowly.

"You've got to be fucking kidding me, right?" she said sharply.

"I've played second fiddle before, Jocelyn. I never intend to do it again," Sable said, her voice strong.

"Did you just call me Jocelyn?" Jocelyn asked evenly.

"Yeah, I did." Sable's look indicated that she didn't care if Jocelyn liked it or not.

Jocelyn made a disgusted noise in the back of her throat. "I have news for you, sweetheart—you were first chair all the way, and you fucked it up by overthinking it."

Shock was evident on Sable's face. Jocelyn got off the freeway to head up to the house.

"Yeah, see?" Jocelyn said, making a circling motion with her index finger. "This, this shit right here, is some serious fucking lesbian bullshit. This is the shit that fucks everything up… fucking overthinking shit and thinking you know what I'm thinking without even asking one fucking question. So fucking classic! I fucking hate that shit!"

Sable blinked, surprised by Jocelyn's vehemence.

"And you!" Jocelyn said, stabbing a finger at Sable. "I'm not fucking Gage, okay? I wouldn't have screwed you over like that, ever!"

Sable swallowed hard as she realized that she'd made a mistake where Jocelyn was concerned. Jocelyn pulled into the garage and got out of her car, storming into the house. Sable followed after her, not sure what to do or say. Jocelyn went straight to her room and sat down on the bed, her booted foot on the bed, one arm looped over her knee. Sable walked into the room meekly, hoping that Jocelyn had calmed down a bit. No such luck.

"And are you fucking kidding me? Gage? Really?" Jocelyn snapped. "How many fucking times did I tell you that she and I are just friends? Just fucking friends!"

"Fucking friends—that's the key there," Sable said triumphantly.

Jocelyn narrowed her eyes dangerously at Sable. "You're really going to pull that shit with me?" she asked, her tone as low and threatening as her look.

They regarded each other for a long moment, then Jocelyn shook her head.

"For your fucking information, I haven't been with Gage since I was with you. Not once, and do you know why?"

"Why?" Sable asked softly.

"Because she has Kit, and I want her to have Kit. She's in love with the girl, and that's all I've ever wanted for my best friend. I didn't want to be the one she was with; I just wanted her to have a life."

Sable pressed her lips together, her eyes indicating that she was starting to understand her mistake.

Jocelyn gave another mirthless laugh and leaned back against the headboard.

"And I'll be totally honest with you, Sable," she said. "For the first few months that you were gone… Yeah, it fucked me up."

"But?" Sable asked hesitantly.

"But," Jocelyn said, her lips curling nastily, "I'm sorry, sweetheart, you got upstaged." Her voice held so much angst that Sable moved closer to her.

"What do you mean?"

"I mean, you got replaced, exchanged, supplanted," Jocelyn said, her voice almost a growl.

"By another woman." Sable had heard from Cat about the blonde at the Club.

Jocelyn laughed, and the hair on the back of Sable's neck stood up at the hollow, gut-wrenching sound.

"Yeah, another woman," Jocelyn said snidely.

Sable nodded, looking devastated.

Jocelyn saw the look and sighed, shaking her head slowly.

"I have cancer, Sable," Jocelyn said, so simply that Sable stared at her in mute shock for a long minute.

"What!" Sable breathed, looking sick suddenly.

Sable sat on the bed near Jocelyn's foot, like all the fight had left her suddenly.

"Yeah," Jocelyn said, her gaze level.

"Oh my God…" Sable closed her eyes.

Jocelyn saw the devastation on her face and felt it really hit her again. As long as she could pretend she didn't know it, it was easier to forget. Seeing someone react to the news only made it real again.

"How… when…?"

"How when, what?" Jocelyn asked evenly.

43

"How long have you known?"

"About a month now."

"And Gage doesn't know?" Sable asked, thinking that Gage hadn't seemed to know when she'd called her.

"No," Jocelyn said, "and that's the way it's going to stay."

"Why wouldn't you tell her?" Sable asked.

"Did you hear what I said earlier? She's in love with Kit, her life is moving forward finally… I'm not going to fuck that up with this bull-shit," Jocelyn said gruffly.

"What?" Sable queried. "If nothing else, how are you going to take the time you'll need for treatment? She's your boss."

Jocelyn simply looked back at Sable, her face telling Sable every-thing. And suddenly she understood. It hit her almost physically; Jocelyn had no intention of fighting.

"You're not getting treatment, are you?" Sable asked in a devas-tated whisper, tears in her eyes.

"No," Jocelyn said. "I don't see the point."

"The point is that people love you, Jocelyn!" Sable exclaimed.

"Yeah," Jocelyn said. "And I don't intend for the people I love to suffer right along with me until I die anyway."

"People survive cancer all the time."

"Not people that live the way I do," Jocelyn countered hotly.

"That's it, isn't it?" Sable said. "The risky behavior? You're hoping to die in some fiery crash, so they'll never know…"

Jocelyn's level look answered that question effectively.

"You can't…" Sable said, the tears in her eyes spilling over as she shook her head.

"Oh, you'd be surprised what I can do when I put my mind to it," Jocelyn said wryly.

"Then put your fucking mind to fighting this!" Sable snapped, her dark eyes flashing angrily.

Jocelyn's eyes widened at Sable's exclamation. "Sable…" she began in a placating tone.

"No!" Sable said, making a cutting gesture with her hand. "Don't try to explain to me how you're going to let yourself die. I'm not going to listen to that bullshit! You are going to fucking fight this, Jocelyn Mann, or I swear to God I'm going to fucking kick your ass!"

Jocelyn stared back at Sable searchingly.

Sable pulled out her phone and started tapping at the screen.

"What are you doing?" Jocelyn asked mildly.

"What kind of cancer is it?" Sable asked, not looking up at Jocelyn.

"Ovarian," Jocelyn said. "Apparently if you don't use what the little fuckers produce, they get pissed off and revolt."

A smile tugged at Sable's lips at that description, even as she tapped out the letters. After a few long moments, Sable sat next to Jocelyn on the bed, holding her phone still and reading.

"Okay, so this says that you need to have a laparotomy to determine if it's really cancer."

"They told me it's cancer," Jocelyn said.

"So they already tested the tumor?" Sable said.

"Yeah."

"How'd you manage that without Gage knowing?"

"Talent," Jocelyn responded shortly.

Sable narrowed her eyes at Jocelyn. "You had surgery?"

"To check out the tumor," Jocelyn said. "And they confirmed it's cancer."

"Okay," Sable said, nodding. "This says that they need to basically do a total hysterectomy. Did you manage that feat under Gage's nose too?"

Jocelyn tilted her head at Sable. "That would be treatment, babe, and that would be followed by a hellacious course of chemo that I'm not interested in suffering through."

"Too bad. You're going to do it," Sable said simply.

"Guess again," Jocelyn replied.

Sable turned to Jocelyn, her face serious. "You will, or I'll go and tell Gage everything right now and she'll make you do it."

"No one makes me do anything, sweetheart," Jocelyn said sharply.

Sable's eyes searched Jocelyn's. It took a good long look, but Sable saw the fear there.

"You're afraid..." she said gently.

"Fucking terrified," Jocelyn said, her voice tremulous suddenly as her lips trembled.

There were tears in Sable's eyes instantly. She'd never seen Jocelyn completely vulnerable, and it affected her deeply. She put her arms around Jocelyn, half expecting her to push away, but she didn't. To Sable's utter shock, Jocelyn crumbled against her, and Sable could feel her shaking. In that moment Sable's determination doubled. She was not letting this woman give up. She didn't care what it took, she was going to get Jocelyn through this.

"We can fight this, Jocelyn," Sable said, holding Jocelyn against her, her hand at Jocelyn's head. "I will be with you, if you'll let me... I'll be with you every step of the way."

She felt Jocelyn shudder, but then, to her amazement, Sable felt her nod. She hugged Jocelyn tighter, knowing that this was what had pushed her to come back.

She'd been in London when Gage had called her. She'd also been in the middle of a recording session that had taken a lot of time to get out of. What had scared her was when Gage had said that she was afraid she'd be burying Jocelyn in the next couple of months if something didn't change. That thought had changed Sable's thought processes immediately. Yes, she'd been very hurt by what Jocelyn had said that night in Gage's bedroom, and she'd felt like history had been repeating itself. The fact was, though, that if she hadn't already been emotionally attached to Jocelyn, it wouldn't have hurt that much, and she knew that. For whatever reason, Jocelyn Mann, with her strong opinions and attitude, had wormed her way right into Sable's heart. The sex certainly hadn't been anything to sneeze at either—it had been earth shattering, and Sable had quickly found herself addicted. She'd been completely bereft when she'd left California.

"The first thing we need to do is get you healthy," Sable said gently. "I don't know how much weight you've lost, but it's way too much. Are you eating at all?"

"Nothing stays down," Jocelyn said, her head still against Sable's chest, her body resting against Sable's.

"Okay, so we do something about that first."

Jocelyn made a noise in the back of her throat. "Like?"

"Well, there's always pot," Sable said, grinning.

"Now that it's legal?" Jocelyn asked, and Sable could feel her grin too.

"Yeah," Sable said, "and I've heard that cops always know where to get the best stuff."

Jocelyn actually chuckled. "If I was still in San Francisco, I would."

"Well, I can definitely get ahold of some. Jake will have contacts."

"Jake?" Jocelyn sat up, sliding her arms around Sable and keeping her close.

"He's my bodyguard. You'll like him." Sable snuggled against Jocelyn, feeling the familiarity with her again quickly.

"Oh, this is the guy whose mother died, right?" Jocelyn asked.

Sable nodded.

"How's he doing?" Jocelyn asked.

"He's okay," Sable said. "Back to his usual self."

"Which is?"

"Oh, you need to meet him to truly understand," Sable said, a smile playing at her lips.

"Oh, goodie," Jocelyn said. "So where is he now?"

"Probably parked outside in the drive," Sable said, grinning.

"Uh…" Jocelyn murmured, confused.

"He would have followed us from the office. He rarely lets me out of his sight."

"He followed me?" Jocelyn looked stunned.

"Probably cussing in Gaelic the entire time because of how fast you were driving."

Jocelyn shook her head. "Gotta be more observant," she muttered.

Jocelyn got up from the bed, taking Sable's hand and pulling her up.

"What are we doing?" Sable asked, looking surprised.

"We're not gonna let the guy sit in the driveway. Jesus…"

"He's used to it."

"Don't care." Jocelyn led Sable out of the bedroom and back toward the front door. She opened it and looked at Sable. "Go get him," she said with a grin on her lips.

Sure enough, Jake was sitting in the black SUV he'd rented for their time in Los Angeles. As Sable walked out of the house, Jake got out of the vehicle. She walked over and talked to him for a moment; Jocelyn stood leaning against the doorjamb, waiting for them. She saw Sable gesture to the house. Jake looked toward the house then back at Sable, shaking his head. Sable gestured back toward where Jocelyn stood, and she could see Jake look directly at her, nodding. Finally Sable started walking back toward the house; Jake locked up the SUV and followed her.

As Sable reached the stairs, Jake caught up to her.

Jocelyn extended her hand to Jake, giving him a direct look.

"Gun," Jocelyn said, nodding to Jake.

"Jake," the bodyguard replied. "You're hard to keep up with," he told her with a smile, his Irish accent clear.

"I didn't know I was being followed." Jocelyn gestured for Jake to come into the house.

Jake grinned. "Would it have mattered?"

"I probably would have gone faster," Jocelyn admitted, grinning back.

"That's what I thought," Jake said.

Jocelyn led them into the kitchen, glancing over at Jake as she reached into the refrigerator. "You want a beer? I'm pretty sure... yes... Lenna keeps Guinness in here."

"Oh," Jake said, looking very tempted.

"Go ahead," Sable said to her bodyguard. "I'm not going anywhere tonight. However, Jocelyn and I have some things to discuss, so take that beer and go find something to do. I promise I won't leave the house."

Jocelyn handed Jake a Guinness, which he took gratefully.

"Jake, make yourself at home. There's a game room downstairs with a pool table, darts, all kinds of shit—and, more importantly, a widescreen," she said with a wink.

"Brilliant." Jake gave Sable a pointed look. "You don't go anywhere outside."

"I won't," Sable assured him.

"Is the back okay?" Jocelyn asked. "I need a cigarette in the worst way right now."

"Let me check it out first," Jake said.

"Okay. Sable, show him where it's at. I need to grab my cigarettes."

Ten minutes later, Sable and Jocelyn were outside on the porch that overlooked the city of Los Angeles. Jocelyn sat in one of the chairs and lit a cigarette, taking a deep draw.

"Should you really be smoking?" Sable asked, perching on the low stone railing of the outside patio, facing Jocelyn.

"It's not lung cancer," Jocelyn replied drily.

Sable nodded, knowing she shouldn't annoy Jocelyn too much at this point.

"We should talk about next steps though," she said softly.

Jocelyn nodded, taking another deep drag on her cigarette, her eyes ranging out over the view, her jaw set in agitation.

"It sounds like the first thing we need to do is get ahold of your doctor and get the laparotomy scheduled," Sable said.

Jocelyn winced but nodded. "Does it say how long it takes to recover?"

"Let me check," Sable said. "This says that it could be as little as three days, unless there are complications. I'd count on about a week."

Jocelyn inhaled deeply. "I'm not going to be able to hide that," she said, her face pensive.

"You need to tell Gage, Jocelyn."

"Will you stop calling me that?" Jocelyn snapped.

Sable looked at her for a long moment. "You need to tell her," she said, knowing that was the part Jocelyn really didn't want to hear.

"You don't get it," Jocelyn said. "You don't know her like I do."

"Tell me," Sable said.

"Gage needs to save people; she needs to be the knight in shining armor. If I tell her this, she'll literally drop her entire life to fix me."

"And you think that would include Kit?"

Jocelyn shrugged. "I don't know. She's never been in love before, so I don't know for sure, but I do know I'm not taking that chance."

Sable drew in a deep breath. Jocelyn was only solidifying what she'd said earlier, that she wanted Gage with Kit, and not her. Sable realized again how foolish she'd been in running out on Jocelyn. She wondered if Jocelyn would have been less reluctant to get treatment if they'd still been together originally. With that thought in mind, Sable kneeled in front of Jocelyn, looking up at her and putting her hands on Jocelyn's jean-clad thighs.

"I'm sorry," she said sincerely.

Jocelyn looked back down at her, her eyes searching. "For what?"

"For leaving," Sable answered. "For not trusting you enough to talk to you about what I thought."

Jocelyn looked at her again, then, stubbing out her cigarette, leaned forward to touch Sable's face, her eyes gazing into Sable's.

"I'm not Cat," Jocelyn said. "I'm not in love with anyone else."

Sable desperately wanted to ask if that meant that Jocelyn was in love with her, but she didn't want to push. Her heart, however, leaped

51

at the possibility. To cover her fluster, Sable shifted upward, capturing Jocelyn's lips with her own. Jocelyn's hand slid from her cheek to the back of her neck, pulling her closer as she deepened the kiss. Sable's hands moved to Jocelyn's shoulders as she straddled Jocelyn's lap, their lips still connected hungrily. Jocelyn moved her other hand to Sable's waist, pulling at her, drawing her closer.

When things got particularly heated, Jocelyn stood, carefully setting Sable on her feet. It dragged at her that normally she'd have been able to carry the smaller woman back to her room. Cancer sucked. Instead she took Sable's hand and led her back into the house and to her room.

Inside the room she began kissing Sable again, reaching up to pull off the shirt that Sable wore; Sable moved to do the same. She saw the small bandage on Jocelyn's abdomen just below her belly button when she unbuttoned Jocelyn's jeans to push them off.

In minutes they were both naked and Jocelyn was laying Sable down on her bed, moving over her, kissing her hungrily as she did. Sable's hands pulled at Jocelyn, having missed her body so much. She hadn't been with anyone since she'd left, so when Jocelyn's body pressed against her, she was so ready she came immediately. Jocelyn continued to kiss her lips, sliding her hand between them to touch her. She brought Sable to orgasm two more times before moving down her body.

Jocelyn's lips touched her skin in warm, wet kisses, her hands trailing after her mouth as she moved down, touching, caressing, and making Sable moan over and over again. When Jocelyn's mouth touched her inner thigh, Sable tensed, waiting. Jocelyn slid her hands up Sable's thighs, pressing her legs apart, and Sable was sure she'd come then. Then Jocelyn took her time, her tongue touching, probing, exciting her just to the brink, but then stopping. Sable was begging, her hands in Jocelyn's hair.

"Please..."

Jocelyn lowered her head, her mouth closing over a hard clit and sucking. Sable screamed so loud it was a wonder Jake didn't come running in with his gun drawn. Apparently he was used to Sable's appetites, so that didn't happen.

As Jocelyn lay next to Sable, Sable decided to get back some of her own and moved her body over Jocelyn's. Within moments Jocelyn was coming and holding on to Sable's hips, grinding them against her.

Afterwards they lay together trying to catch their breath.

"If I want to get away with any of this," Jocelyn said, still slightly out of breath, "I need to get out of this house..." Her voice trailed off in thought.

Sable nodded. "I can find us a house."

"*You* can?" Jocelyn asked. "I said *I* need to..."

"Yeah," Sable said, levering herself up on her elbow. "And if you want it to happen fast in LA, you need money. I have lots."

Jocelyn looked back at her mutinously.

"Jocelyn, let me do this for you, please?" Sable said. "Put aside your butch pride for a minute, okay?"

Jocelyn couldn't help but grin at that comment.

"Okay, you're right," she said.

"Good. I'll get my agent looking right away."

A week later, everyone was shocked that not only was Sable apparently back, but that she and Jocelyn were now so officially a couple that they'd bought a house and moved in together in that time.

"Second-date U-Haul thing, huh?" Sebastian commented to Gage when they heard about Jocelyn's sudden relationship status change.

"Ya think?" Kashena said, rolling her eyes from where she sat in Gage's office.

"I know, I'm actually pretty shocked myself," Gage said. "But if she stops trying to kill herself off, I'm happy."

"Yeah, did I hear right that you almost pitted her Viper?" Sebastian asked.

"Yep."

"She'd have killed you," Sebastian said, shaking his head.

"Well, she got out of it anyway. I'm just glad she didn't end up dead." Gage said, sighing.

"And now they're on vacation for a week?" Kashena asked.

"Yeah," Gage said. "Hey, if it gets her head screwed back on straight, I'm fine with it."

Sebastian and Kashena both nodded.

***

Shenin got up, took a shower, and began getting ready. It had been a month since she'd had the baby, and it was time to get back to work. It took a couple of tries to find something to wear. It bugged her that nothing really fit right at that point. She was still feeling as big as a house, and she hated it. Tyler accidentally walked right into her ire.

"That looks comfortable," Tyler said, smiling as she leaned against the bathroom door with Aiden in her arms.

Shenin threw her a vile look. "Great, that's exactly what I was going for," she said, going back to putting her makeup on.

"Babe…" Tyler sensed Shenin's mood but didn't step the right way to get out of it. "You just had a baby—you can't expect to be perfect yet."

Shenin's green eyes flashed. "Yeah, thanks." Her tone was far from grateful as she went back to her makeup.

Tyler knew she'd said exactly the wrong thing, and she also knew that trying to fix it would only make things worse. She walked out of the bathroom, taking Aiden with her.

"Mommy was just really stupid," Tyler told Aiden as she sat down on the bed, laying him in front of her. "And she's likely not going to get laid again for the next year or so," she said, winking.

Aiden gurgled and kicked his feet.

"I'm not sensing any sort of sympathy here, dude," Tyler said, grinning at the baby.

Twenty minutes later, Shenin emerged from the bathroom. She walked over to the bed and leaned down to kiss Aiden, then looked at Tyler.

"There's bottles in the fridge, and don't forget the stuff for diaper rash. He's really hatin' life with this humidity," Shenin said.

"I got it, babe. We'll be fine, I promise." Tyler touched Shenin's face. "I love you," she said softly.

"I love you," Shenin repeated, nodding. "I gotta go. Have fun, you two."

As Shenin left the room, Tyler looked down at Aiden.

"Okay, maybe a year and a half…"

Later, at the office, Shenin met with Gage. In the time that Shenin had been gone, her assistant had gotten another job and moved to San Diego.

"I really hate to do it, Shen, but I gotta assign you Kimber for the time being," Gage said, grimacing.

"It's fine, Gage," Shenin said. "She's never said one flirtatious thing to me. I think I'm safe." She winked at Gage.

"It's Kimber I'm worried about," Gage said with a grin. "She comes on to you and Tyler's going to rip her lungs out. And that's at the very least a lot of workers' comp paperwork."

Shenin laughed, shaking her head. "You're terrible."

A few minutes later, she was in her office when Kimber knocked on the door.

"Come on in," Shenin said, motioning for her to come in and sit down.

Kimber walked in, looking very nervous.

Shenin smiled. "Have a seat."

Kimber sat down. "Look, I know what you've heard about me, and—"

"Relax," Shenin told the girl. "I'm not going off what people are saying. I know full well that Gun is an adult, and she participated fully in whatever you two had going on. As far as I'm concerned, what happened between you two is her business and yours, okay?"

Kimber nodded slowly, seeming surprised by what Shenin had said.

"Further, the thing with Harley… Well, we'll chalk that up to you being young and not knowing any better."

Kimber bit her lip, looking relieved but still worried.

"You and I will start with a clean slate, okay?" Shenin said.

Kimber blinked a few times, then nodded.

"But I'm telling you," Shenin continued, "what everyone is saying about my wife is very true. If you even blink wrong in my direction and Tyler hears about it, she'll kill you slowly and painfully."

Kimber's eyes widened as she swallowed, then she saw Shenin start to grin.

"I guess now wouldn't be the time to tell you that you look pretty damned good for a woman that just had a baby a month ago?" Kimber said, smiling.

"Probably not," Shenin said, winking at the girl.

"Fine." Kimber sighed. "I'll keep that to myself."

Shenin chuckled.

"So where do you want to start first?" Kimber asked then. "I was working on updating the files you and Shelly were starting with—do you want to see that?"

"Yeah, that sounds like a good place to start."

"Okay, I'll go grab what I have."

Later that afternoon, Kimber was sitting at her desk outside Shenin's office when Tyler walked up with Aiden in her arms.

Kimber looked up, seeing Tyler and catching the narrowing of Tyler's blue eyes.

"Hi." Kimber smiled. "You're Tyler, right?" she said, doing her best to be extra nice.

She was very curious about this woman—with everything she'd heard, she'd never actually seen Tyler Hancock. The day the baby had been born, she hadn't been able to get close enough to see Tyler. Now, she could see that she had an all-American down-home look to her, but there was a very definite dangerous glint in her eyes. She did exude a kind of strength and command presence that spoke to what people had warned her about. She was, however, really good-looking, and Kimber could see how Shenin would be attracted to her.

"Yeah," Tyler said. "And you are?"

"I'm Kimber," she said, smiling.

Tyler's eyes narrowed again, this time more dangerously, and Kimber knew that Tyler had heard about her.

"Director?" Kimber called, as Tyler took a step toward her.

Tyler smirked, seeing that the girl was afraid of her; she wondered what people had been telling her. Shenin came out of her office, responding to the fear she'd heard in Kimber's voice. She saw Tyler standing there with an amused grin on her lips, looking at Kimber.

"Ty," Shenin chided; she knew Tyler had been trying to intimidate the girl.

"Hi, babe," Tyler said, kissing Shenin on the lips.

"There's my boy!" Shenin said, taking Aiden from Tyler. "Ty, this is Kimber, and stop giving her that look."

Tyler chuckled as she extended her hand to Kimber, her look direct as she did. Kimber extended her hand, and Tyler noted that it was shaking. Good, Tyler thought as she shook Kimber's hand.

After Tyler left, Kimber was in Shenin's office.

"I'm sorry," Shenin said.

"For what?"

"For Ty. She tends to be kind of… intense."

"When it comes to you, it seems," Kimber said. "I understand it— if you were mine I'd probably be pretty intense with other women around you too."

Shenin stared at Kimber, knowing the girl had just flirted with her and knowing she should tell her not to… The words wouldn't come. It felt too good to hear someone say something like that at that moment in time.

She shook her head, going to back to what she was typing on her computer. She didn't see Kimber smile as she walked out of the room.

Chapter 3

Jocelyn had her surgery the day after she and Sable moved into the house Sable had bought.

"You could have rented something, you know," Jocelyn had said, shaking her head.

Sable had shrugged. "I can always use a house in Los Angeles."

Jocelyn had signed over power of attorney to Sable, in case something went wrong during the surgery. Sable hadn't been pleased with what she considered Jocelyn's negativity but had agreed to it all the same.

As Sable waited in the private waiting room at Cedars Sinai, she saw Finley Taylor walk by. She ducked her head slightly; if Finley saw her, she might start checking as to what was going on. Sable sincerely hoped that Finley didn't see her. She wasn't so lucky.

"Someone told me you were here," Finley said, walking into the waiting room a few minutes later. "Is everything okay?"

Sable nodded, looking nervous.

"Sable, I can't say anything to anyone," Finley told her.

"So you already know?"

"I overheard the surgeon talking about it. Don't worry, okay?"

"Jocelyn doesn't want Gage to find out."

"I won't say a word to anyone, I promise. Not even Kai, okay?" Finley said. "How are you doing with all of this?" She sat down next to Sable.

"Scared to death," Sable said honestly.

"Well, I can tell you that she'll be fine. The surgeon she's got is one of the best. He'll make sure he gets everything. She is going to do chemo though, right?" Finley asked.

"I'm hoping so," Sable said, her lips trembling.

Finley studied Sable for a long moment. "Is this whole thing with you two suddenly being a couple a ruse to hide this from Gage?"

Sable shrugged. "I don't really know. I know Jocelyn wants to keep Gage from knowing about the cancer, and she's letting me help her, but I really don't know how she feels…"

Finley gave her a long look. "You're in love with her, aren't you?"

Sable drew in a deep breath and let it out slowly, nodding almost miserably.

Finley nodded too. "Well, it's really amazing of you to be here for her during this. We were all worried as hell about her—we had no idea what had sent her spinning. We figured it was the breakup with you… but this… this makes sense too."

"I guess it was a little bit of both," Sable said.

"Well, stick by her, Sable. She really needs you right now, whether she realizes it or not. And if you need anything," Finley said as she stood, "call me." She handed Sable her card with her cell phone number on the back. "No matter what time, okay?"

"Thank you," Sable said, relieved to have someone with actual medical training that she could contact if something came up.

Finley left. Half an hour later, Sable was told that the surgery had gone well and that Jocelyn was awake and asking for her.

Walking into the hospital room, she saw Jocelyn lying in the bed with her eyes closed. She sat down in the chair next to the bed. Jocelyn stirred immediately.

"Hi," Sable said, smiling.

"Hey," Jocelyn said, smiling slightly too.

"How are you feeling?"

"Like hell, thanks for asking," Jocelyn said in an overly bright voice.

"Are you in pain?" Sable stood up to look Jocelyn over.

"Yeah, some."

"I can call the nurse…"

"It's okay."

"Okay," Sable said.

To her surprise, Jocelyn held out her hand to her. Sable took Jocelyn's hand in hers, smiling down at her.

"They said it went well," Sable told her.

Jocelyn nodded, looking serious. "They still want me to do chemo though."

"We thought they probably would, babe. This isn't a surprise," Sable said softly.

"I know," Jocelyn said. "But I guess part of me was hoping they'd get in there and say 'Oh hell, we were wrong, you're fine.'"

Sable folded her lips together in a slight grimace. She kissed Jocelyn gently. "We'll figure it out."

"Chemo's gonna be harder than hell to hide, Sable," Jocelyn said. "I'm only going to get away with so many 'vacations' before Gage kills me herself."

"They're going to want you to start right away too," Sable said. "They want to make sure that anything they didn't get in the surgery gets annihilated fast."

Jocelyn nodded, her face grave.

"We'll figure it out," Sable said again.

"I hope you're right."

***

61

"Okay, so exactly where am I going?" Sydney asked Harley.

"Just follow the bois," Harley said, grinning.

It was Sydney's birthday, and the Lost Bois had plans for her.

"I can't believe you're letting Shiloh drive your car," Sydney said.

Harley smiled widely. "It's not far."

"Jesus, where are we going?" Sydney asked again.

"Sorry, can't tell ya."

"You suck, boss." Sydney grinned.

"Bangarang," Harley said, laughing. "So she's running good, huh?" Harley asked then, referring to Sydney's latest acquisition, a bright metallic green 1995 300ZX twin turbo.

"Yeah," Sydney said, smiling brightly. "After that last tune, she's running really good. Thanks to you and the bois."

"I told you—stick with us, we'll help ya out."

"Why is Cody riding her Ninja?" Sydney asked, surprised at seeing Cody's bike in the lineup, since everyone else was in cars. "I thought McKenna was coming."

"She is; she's in with Dakota and Jazmine. Cody's been having tuning issues with her bike, so she's riding it to try to work some bugs out before our next run."

"Oh, okay, makes sense."

"You need to get a bike," Harley said.

"Well, I can't afford one like yours," Sydney said, grinning. "I might get a Shadow or something."

"That would be cool too."

They were both silent for a bit, then Sydney broached a subject she'd been chewing on for a while.

"So, hey, did you notice that guy flirting with Shy today?" Sydney asked.

"Huh?" Harley queried. "Which guy?"

Sydney looked over at the other woman, openmouthed. "You didn't, did you? The guy from LA Fire that was in the office today."

Harley simply looked back at her blankly.

"Jesus, dude, he was all up on her," Sydney said.

"Shy's not into guys, Syd."

"You willing to bet Shy on that?"

"You're nuts," Harley said, shaking her head. "Shy loves me."

"Okay, but I'm saying you need to make sure you keep an eye on that kind of shit," Sydney said. "You said she's been getting annoyed at how much you hang with the bois... You might want to start paying more attention to your girl."

Harley stared at Sydney, surprised by the conversation.

"Oh, what the hell?" Sydney said as they pulled into a parking lot of a club called the Body Shop; it was a strip club. "You gotta be kidding me..."

Harley chuckled as Sydney parked her car, looking supremely embarrassed already.

"I'll warn ya now, Jet's buying you a lap dance," Harley told her as she got out of the car.

Sydney banged her head over and over on the new neochrome steering wheel she'd just installed on the Z that morning. She set her forehead against it and shook her head, finally sighing and climbing out of the car.

"I hate you people," Sydney said as she got out of the car to a great deal of ribbing from the group.

All of the Lost Bois and their girlfriends or wives were there to celebrate Sydney's birthday.

"Come on, Syd," Jet said. "Do you know how fast I had to talk to get Fadi to come?"

"I am still sure it is not a good idea," Fadiyah said, rolling her eyes at her wife.

"I'm with you, Fadi." Sydney nodded to Fadiyah. "Let's go," she said, grinning.

Fadiyah laughed and took a step toward Sydney.

"Don't make me have to shoot Syd on her own birthday, babe," Jet said, narrowing her light-green eyes at Sydney.

"Let's go." Skyler nodded toward the club. "Sydney, you are going to drink and watch half-naked girls dance."

"And get a lap dance, or two," Dakota added.

Sydney dropped her head but followed the group to the front doors of the club.

Mia noticed the group right away—who could miss them? A group of no less than fifteen women and not an ugly one in the group. It had spread quickly among the dancers that they were damned good tippers. Surveying the group as she danced on the stage near them, she noticed the one who constantly lowered her eyes, pressing her lips together as she shook her head. Mia found herself watching her, because it was obvious that she was embarrassed at being there. It was also obvious that her friends were the ones that had dragged her there; they were all buying her drinks and toasting her.

Mia took note of the black skinny jeans, the white high-top tennis shoes, the black tank top with a white button-up shirt over it, and the black-and-white ball cap worn backward. Around her neck Mia could make out a black corded necklace; she also wore a studded watchband at her wrist and a few silver rings.

Mia decided the girl was actually kind of cute. Her smile, when she smiled, was shy but very engaging. She also caught the girl looking at her a few times. Mia found herself purposely trying to catch the girl's gaze, and when she did, she smiled sweetly at her, giving her a wink.

Sydney noticed the beautiful girl smiling at her. She had a seriously nice body, her hair was a pastel rainbow, and she had the biggest blue eyes Sydney had ever seen. She couldn't help but watch her dance; the girl did so in such a way that Sydney's eyes were drawn to her over and over again. One time the girl was looking directly at her, and she saw the girl smile at her and wink. Sydney squeezed her eyes shut in embarrassment, opening just one to see if the girl was still looking at her. She was, and the beautiful rainbow-haired girl laughed slightly, smiling at Sydney again.

Jet and Skyler exchanged glances, having noticed that Sydney was watching the cute girl with the rainbow hair. Then they saw the exchange between the two and knew they needed to work a little magic.

"Okay, Syd," Jet said, handing Sydney another shot of Casa Noble tequila. "Time for you to pick a girl for your lap dance."

"No," Sydney said. "There's no way… I wouldn't have a clue what to do."

Skyler smirked. "Oh, it'll come to ya."

It took another twenty minutes and another shot of tequila to get Sydney to not only agree to a lap dance, but to pick a girl. Predictably, she picked the girl with the rainbow hair, whose stage name was Rainbow.

"It's fate." Jet winked at Sydney as she walked her into the private room where the lap dances were done.

"I hate you so hard right now."

Jet put her tongue between her teeth and waggled her eyebrows. "Have fun," she said, winking.

On her way out, Jet saw the girl wearing a tiny silver-and-white G-string and bikini. Jet pressed a bill into the girl's hand.

"This is her first lap dance," Jet said, her lips right next to the girl's ear. "Make it a good one, will ya?"

The girl looked down at the bill in her hand, and her eyes widened when she saw that it was a hundred. She looked up at Jet, blinking a couple of times. Jet smiled seductively, then walked away.

Mia stared after the dark-haired woman. These women sure did have a way about them, didn't they? She found that she was actually nervous for the first time in a very long time. Taking a deep breath, she walked into the room, looking over at the dark-haired girl, who was standing with her hands in her pockets.

The first thing the girl did was to remove her hat. "Sorry," she said, as if Mia had just said something about the hat.

Mia smiled. "It's okay. I understand this is your first lap dance."

Sydney nodded, looking fairly mortified.

Mia walked over. "Tell you what," she said softly, her blue eyes staring up into Sydney's, "we'll take this nice and slow, and I promise I won't hurt you… much."

She added the last word with a wink.

Sydney laughed quietly, pressing her lips together.

"What's your name?" Mia asked.

"Sydney," the girl replied.

"I'm Mia," Mia said, knowing her boss would kill her for giving her real name, but she really wanted to make this girl comfortable. "Why don't you sit down, Sydney?" She gestured to the chair in the room.

Sydney did what she suggested. Mia noted that she sat with her back rigid, her legs apart but far from relaxed.

"Sydney, this is supposed to be fun, you know," Mia said, smiling.

Sydney laughed again. "Sorry, this is just really… awkward."

Mia smiled. "Well, let's just see what we can do here, okay? First of all, no one is here but you and me, and no one else can see what's going on, so you don't need to be embarrassed. Okay?"

Sydney drew in a deep breath, nodding.

Mia turned on music, hoping that would help Sydney relax. The first song was one that Sydney recognized, because it was one Memphis had put on the Bangarang playlist—"Show Me Love" by Clean Bandit. As Mia started dancing, Sydney found herself watching her. It wasn't overtly sexy, so Sydney simply enjoyed watching the girl move; she certainly could dance. To Sydney it was no different than watching the girls at the Club dance, which she did often.

Mia could see that Sydney was relaxing, and she found that she very much liked having Sydney watch her dance. She could see Sydney moving her head and mouthing the words to the song.

"You know this one?" Mia asked.

"A friend of mine is a DJ; she has this song on her playlist," Sydney said.

"Cool," Mia said, smiling. She moved closer to Sydney as the song changed. "Do you dance?"

"I can," Sydney said, smiling shyly.

"Will you come dance with me?" Mia held her hand out to Sydney.

Sydney gave her an inscrutable look.

"What?" Mia asked, still moving.

"Pretty girl asks you to dance, you dance," she said as she took Mia's hand and stood up.

"Oh... I like that," Mia said, her blue eyes sparkling.

Mia moved closer as the song "Sweat" came on. Sliding her hand up Sydney's chest, Mia shifted her body closer to Sydney's, like she would if they were dancing in a club. Mia found that Sydney wasn't lying about being able to dance; they easily fell into a rhythm together. It was an easy transition to make when the song changed again to a much more seductive song in Spanish, "Perverso" by Tiziano Ferro. It had a dance beat, but it was also a driving seductive rhythm that allowed for a lot of hip movement.

Mia backed Sydney up and eased her down into the chair, straddling her lap, her body hovering a mere inch above Sydney's. Keeping her hand on Sydney's shoulder, Mia gyrated her body against Sydney's, lowering her head so their lips were so close, just a breath away. Mia was shocked at how much she wanted to move that tiny bit and kiss this girl. Sydney's hands were at her waist, but not in a grasping, lecherous way—they were the hands of a lover, and a respectful one at that. Whereas Mia would usually have been freaked out at someone touching her so intimately at the club, she found that she really liked it with Sydney.

Sydney could not take her eyes off this girl, and she knew she was going to be hating life when the dance was over. She sincerely hoped that there was really cold water in the bathrooms here, because she was going to need it. This girl was so incredibly hot, it was insane! One minute they were dancing like they were in the club, and the next thing Sydney knew the girl had her down in the chair and the real lap dance had begun. Sydney was willing to bet her next paycheck that this was not standard format for a lap dance. Not that she was going to complain. It was probably the best twenty minutes of her life thus far.

When the song ended, Mia stepped back. "See? You survived," she said, winking at Sydney.

Sydney chuckled as she stood. "You were amazing," she said softly.

"I'm glad you enjoyed it," Mia said, smiling up at Sydney.

Sydney lowered her head, smiling shyly back.

Mia found herself moving close to Sydney again, getting under her eyes and looking up at her. She touched Sydney's cheek.

"I didn't do too much damage, did I?"

Sydney bit her lower lip as she smiled. "Not too much, no."

Mia nodded. "Good." She glanced over at the door then, knowing she needed to get away from this sweet girl, lest she do something crazy. "You better get out there or your friends are really going to light you up."

"Tell me about it!" Sydney said, laughing, and turned toward the door.

Mia was surprised when Sydney touched her arm gently.

"Thank you," she said, her tone sincere, a soft smile on her lips.

"You're welcome," Mia said.

When Sydney walked out of the room, Mia heard a chorus of "Bangarang!" and saw Sydney shake her head as her friends crowded around her.

As she'd expected, Sydney found that it took a while to calm her body back down. It took a few minutes of cold water in the bathroom, where of course she had company giving her a hard time. Finally she slipped out the back door of the club to smoke. She was trying to get away from the rest of the bois, so she moved to the other side of the dumpsters to do her best to hide.

While she was smoking she heard the back door of the club open. She pressed back against the wall, thinking it might be Jet or Skyler. The last thing she needed was another shot.

She heard voices and relaxed, realizing it was someone else and not her friends. She couldn't hear what was being said, but she could tell it was a man and a woman. Doing her best not to eavesdrop, Sydney continued to smoke. Suddenly she heard the woman's voice rise, and it sounded like she was scared. That had her stepping out from behind the dumpster, looking in the direction of the commotion. It was Mia and a man; the man grabbed her and started to back her up toward the wall. Mia was struggling and telling him to stop.

"Hey!" Sydney yelled, striding over to where they stood. "Let her go!"

The man's head snapped around. Sydney could tell he'd thought there wasn't anyone out there. His eyes looked her over, and she could see he didn't consider her any kind of threat.

"Mind your own business, kid," the man spat.

"No, I don't think I will," Sydney said, moving to intercede.

The man whirled on Sydney, letting Mia go.

"You wanna fuck with me?" the man said, his dark eyes flashing in anger.

Sydney regarded him slowly. The man was at least four inches taller than her; he didn't look very muscular, but looks could be deceiving. She sneered in derision and obvious disgust.

"No thanks," she said disparagingly. "And it doesn't sound like the lady wants your attention either, so just back off."

"Come make me," the man said.

Sydney pressed her lips together in annoyance and strode toward the man. He took a swing at her, but she managed to duck. Coming up with an upper cut, she caught him under the chin. She heard Mia scream, but she was too busy jumping back out of the guy's reach as he made a grab for her. He managed to get a hand on her, and he'd just managed to punch her once in the face and was leveling another punch when Sydney heard the back door open. She was happy to see Harley, who immediately saw what was going on. Sydney wrenched away from the man's grasp as Harley shouted, "Lost Bois!" and then drew her gun from the small of her back.

"Don't even fucking think about touching her again!" Harley yelled, her tone all cop at that moment.

Sydney moved around the man, who'd frozen at the sound of authority in Harley's voice. Sydney grabbed Mia's hand and pulled her back out of the way. Sydney didn't want Mia to get stuck in the middle of any kind of struggle, or whatever ensued. The rest of the Lost Bois came out on the run. Before the man had time to say a word, he had three nasty-looking guns pointed at him, held by some fairly hot but angry lesbians.

Mia stood behind Sydney, her hand still in Sydney's. She was trembling from head to toe. Sydney noticed that the wind was coming up, and Mia only had a T-shirt over what she had been wearing during the lap dance. She unbuttoned her overshirt and wrapped it around Mia as Jet, who held one of the guns, glanced over at her.

"You okay, Syd?" Jet asked.

"Yeah, but he was trying to attack Mia," Sydney said, gesturing to the girl. Mia shifted behind Sydney, her hand finding Sydney's again and clasping it tight.

Jet's eyes narrowed dangerously at the man. She looked over at Sydney again.

"Looks like he got one in. You want to press charges?" Jet asked, raising a black eyebrow.

"Charges?" the man croaked. "You're cops?"

A slow, evil grin bloomed on Jet's face as she reached into her back pocket and pulled out her badge, holding it up to the man.

"Son of a… Fuck!" the man snapped, throwing a dirty look at Mia as if she'd somehow planned this. "You fucking cunt!" he yelled at her.

Sydney felt Mia shaking, and turned so that Mia was completely behind her. "You might want to show the lady some respect," Sydney said, "since she's the only thing that stands between you and a jail cell for tonight." With that, Sydney turned to Mia and touched her cheek. "Do you want me to press charges?"

Mia wet her lips nervously, her eyes wide. She slowly shook her head, looking scared.

"Are you sure?" Sydney asked.

Mia nodded as she swallowed convulsively.

Sydney turned to the man again. "You're in luck, she's feeling generous," she said, her tone indicating that she didn't agree with Mia's "generosity."

"Get the fuck out of here and never come near her again," Sydney said, her gold eyes blazing with anger and malice.

The man moved past the women standing at the back door, edging by them amidst dirty and still-threatening looks.

Sydney turned to Mia as the bois followed the man inside and made sure he left the club.

"Are you okay?" Sydney asked her.

Sydney could see that it suddenly hit Mia what had happened, or what could have if Sydney hadn't intervened. She put her arm out to support Mia as she sagged a little.

"Oh, my God… he could have… he was going to…"

"Okay, but he didn't," Sydney said, leading her toward the door to the club. "Come on, let's get a couple of shots into you, okay?"

Mia nodded numbly, letting Sydney lead her inside. Sydney took her to the back bar off to the side, asking the bartender for a drink for Mia. The bartender had already seen the rather pointed frog-march of Mia's ex out of the bar, so she knew exactly what Mia needed. She poured Mia a double shot of whiskey and handed it to her. Mia drank the shot, setting the empty glass on the bar and nodding her thanks to the bartender.

"How are you now?" Sydney asked.

"Me?" Mia asked, looking shocked, as she reached up to touch Sydney's cheek, which was bleeding from where the man had hit her. "You're the one bleeding."

Sydney shook her head. "I'm fine."

"You okay?" Harley walked up to the two of them, her eyes surveying Sydney's face with worry.

"Yeah," Sydney said.

"Mia." The manager came up. "I heard what happened. Are you okay?"

"Thanks to these ladies and their friends, yeah," Mia said, gesturing to Sydney and Harley.

The manager looked at Harley and Sydney; he knew that they and their friends had been there for a few hours that night and that every waitress and dancer was in love with them for one reason or another. They were apparently big flirts and also great tippers, as well as highly respectful.

"Thank you," the manager said. "Next round is on me." He looked at Mia again. "You should go home, okay? Does he still have a key to your place?"

Apparently that hadn't occurred to Mia, because she blanched immediately. "Oh God…"

"We'll make sure she gets home safe and that he's not waiting for her," Harley told the manager, giving Sydney an odd grin.

A half hour later, Sydney was standing by her car smoking, waiting for Mia. She'd been told that she needed to be the one to escort Mia home, since all the other Lost Bois were attached and would therefore get skinned if they tried to volunteer. That was backed up by comments from Devin and Jazmine about killing their women if they even thought about it. Sydney was fairly certain she was being

73

set up, but she also knew that Mia needed to be safe, so it was worth it to play the patsy this time.

Mia walked out to the parking lot, with Jet and Fadiyah walking with her.

"Ya good, Syd?" Jet asked, giving her a long look.

"Yeah, I'm fine," Sydney said, knowing Jet was asking about whether or not she was okay to drive.

Sydney opened the passenger door for Mia. As Mia got into the low-slung Z, she saw Jet and Sydney clasp hands.

"Bangarang," Jet said. "Good job tonight."

"Bangarang," Sydney replied.

Sydney got into the car, the look she gave Mia somewhat shy now. "So, tell me where I'm going."

Mia nodded. "If you get to La Cienega you can head south for bit. I'm off of Sunset."

"Okay." Sydney started the car and plugged in her iPhone. Music came on immediately. Sydney winced at the volume and turned it down.

"Sorry," she said, looking embarrassed.

"It's okay," Mia said, seeing that Sydney was being shy again. "It is your car; you're allowed to have your music on." She winked at Sydney.

Sydney smiled bashfully.

Mia was beginning to wonder if this woman was always shy, but right about that time, Sydney changed. As she gunned the engine of the Z and pulled out into traffic, Sydney looked extremely comfortable clutching and shifting the sports car, her hand tapping on the steering wheel to the beat of the song playing on the stereo. The display said it was named "Bangarang." The music was varied and hard edged, and Sydney moved her head with the music, tapping out the beat on the steering wheel.

When the song ended, Mia looked over at Sydney, suddenly noting the gauges in her ears. The girl was definitely edgy, but that was at odds with the shyness Mia had seen in the club. She wasn't sure which one was really Sydney.

"So, bangarang," Mia said.

Sydney licked her lips, grinning. "It's a thing."

"From that movie *Hook*, right? That and Lost Boys?"

"Yeah," Sydney said, "but it's not boys like b-o-y-s, it's boys like b-o-i-s."

"Why?" Mia asked.

Sydney glanced over at her, seeing the open curiosity on Mia's face. "It's kind of a lesbian thing. We're not guys, but they call us butch girls 'bois.'"

"So not to be confused with male boys," Mia said.

"Right."

"And you're all 'lost bois'?" Mia asked. "All the women that were there tonight?"

"No," Sydney said. "Only the more butch ones, like Jet and me."

"And the others?"

"Were girlfriends or wives."

Mia nodded slowly. "But no girlfriend or wife for you?"

Sydney smiled shyly as she shook her head.

"Which is why you got stuck taking me home," Mia said.

Sydney chewed on the inside of her lip, not sure how to answer that. One of the songs that Mia had danced to for Sydney, "Show Me Love," came on the stereo.

"You were not lying," Mia said, laughing happily.

"Nope," Sydney said. "My friend Memphis did this playlist."

"And Memphis is the DJ?" Mia asked, remembering what Sydney had said.

"Yeah."

"And which one was she?" Mia asked, trying to remember all the names and faces that were thrown at her when she'd met the group.

"Short blond hair. She was wearing a blue tank top," Sydney said.

"Oh, yeah, I could see her singing to literally every song they played tonight."

"Yeah, music is her entire world," Sydney said. "She's always sending us all new music, or in some cases she steals some of the girls' phones and adds music herself."

"That's dedication," Mia said. "They don't get pissed at her for that?"

Sydney smiled. "Actually, it's kind of an honor to have her steal your phone at this point. It means she really likes you."

"In a romantic way?" Mia asked.

"Oh, no, she's with Kieran and very happy with her. Memphis is just kind of…" Sydney searched for a way to describe Memphis. "She's really just what one of the American Indians in the group calls a pure spirit. If she likes you, then you're probably a good person."

Mia looked back at Sydney, surprised by what she was saying. "So does she like you?"

Sydney smiled bashfully. "She stole my phone last week at the Club."

"Oh, so she really likes you," Mia said, then tilted her head. "I can see why."

Sydney looked over at Mia speculatively but didn't pursue the conversation.

Mia glanced around at where they were and then hesitantly over at Sydney. Sydney saw it.

"What?" she asked.

"Would you consider me a super big pain in the ass if I asked for a favor?" Mia asked. "I mean, aside from rescuing me and all…"

Sydney chuckled, shaking her head. "Ask, please."

"There's a McDonald's up there before Sawyer—could we stop and grab something? I'm starving."

"Of course."

A couple of minutes later she turned in to the McDonald's parking lot and parked. She walked around and opened the door for Mia, holding her hand out to help her out of the low-slung vehicle. Mia smiled at the very gentlemanly gesture. Sydney also opened the door into the restaurant for her.

When they ordered, Sydney immediately pulled out her wallet, putting her hand gently on Mia's arm to stop her from taking out money. When they were handed cups, Sydney asked her what she wanted and went and got them drinks. Mia could see that this was regular behavior for Sydney; she handed Mia the drinks and went to pick up the tray of food when it was called.

"You're a gentleman," Mia commented as Sydney sat back down.

Sydney smiled at her, her gold eyes sparkling.

"And you have the prettiest eyes," Mia said, finally seeing them in bright light.

Sydney actually blushed as she lowered her gaze.

"And now I've embarrassed you," Mia said, looking at Sydney sideways.

Sydney smiled, reaching for a French fry and eating it while glancing around her.

Mia shook her head. "You weren't shy when you went after Todd earlier," she said. "You were friggin' awesome, actually."

"Was that his name? Todd?"

"Yeah, why?"

Sydney shrugged. "He didn't look like a Todd."

"What did he look like?" Mia asked, curious about how Sydney had seen him.

"Like a Hank or Bart or something equally rednecky," Sydney said.

"Rednecky?" Mia repeated, her blue eyes twinkling humorously.

"Yeah." Sydney grinned. "That's a technical term. You might not understand that," she said with a wink.

Mia laughed, unwrapping her hamburger and taking a bite. Sydney laughed too, and Mia decided she really liked Sydney's laugh.

They sat talking while they ate, and Mia found that when she didn't put Sydney on the spot, or compliment her too much, that Sydney had a really great sense of humor and was also really intelligent.

"So are your friends really cops?" Mia asked.

"Well, Cody and Jet are cops," Sydney said. "Technically Harley isn't anymore, but she still carries."

Mia nodded. "And what do you do?"

"I'm a programmer for OES," Sydney said, taking another French fry.

"OES?"

"Office of Emergency Services," Sydney explained. "Harley's actually my boss."

"Harley is?" Mia asked, surprised. She didn't think Harley looked like a boss, with her long rainbow braids and multiple earrings.

Sydney laughed. "She's actually the deputy director over the IT unit."

"Wow," Mia said, her eyes widening at the impressive title. "What do the others do?"

78

"Well, Jet and Cody work for Department of Justice. So does Sky, she's a pilot. I'm sure you recognized Talon, right?"

"Oh yeah," Mia said, smiling.

"And you know Memphis is a DJ, but she also does music scores for Legend Azaria—you know who that is?"

"She's a big-time director, right?" Mia asked.

"Yeah. Dakota is a contractor, and Kit actually works for Gage, the director of OES. She's also her girlfriend."

Mia blinked in surprise. "I don't think I ever knew how many lesbians there are here in LA."

"Oh, that's nothing; you should meet the rest of the group," Sydney said.

"The rest of the group?"

"Yeah, there's a whole group that hangs out together. We're just a small part of that group," Sydney said, smiling. "There's a couple of rock stars, another movie star, the director of the Division of Law Enforcement, chief legal counsel for OES, various special agent supervisors and agents, another pilot, not counting Gage and Gun who are at OES but also pilots, a retired MMA fighter, a bodyguard, and even Legend Azaria."

"You're really connected," Mia said, her eyes wide.

Sydney laughed. "Yeah, like the lesbian mob or something."

Mia laughed at that.

"You ready?" Sydney asked.

Mia nodded, standing up. Sydney picked up their tray and put the trash on it, taking it over to the trash can.

"Does a girl get to do anything for herself around you?" Mia asked, as Sydney once again opened the door for her on the way out of the restaurant.

"Harley, Jet and Sky are teaching me to be a proper butch," Sydney said with a grin.

"A proper butch?" Mia asked as Sydney opened the car door for her.

"Yeah," Sydney said, smiling softly. "A gentlewoman."

"I think you probably had that down already," Mia said, catching Sydney's quick smile as she closed the door.

A few minutes later they were pulling into Mia's apartment complex.

"You are coming in, right?" Mia asked as Sydney helped her out of the car.

"I was told I was to 'secure the premises,'" Sydney said.

"Good, 'cause I was going to make you come inside anyway," Mia said, winking at her.

"I see," Sydney said with a grin.

She reached into her car and pulled out her phone, then gestured for Mia to lead the way. Mia led Sydney to her apartment and opened the door. Sydney preceded her inside, looking around, her body tense, which told Mia she'd been serious about "securing the premises."

"Everything look okay?" she asked Mia as Mia walked into the apartment. "Nothing out of place, like he's been here?"

Mia looked around; it was essentially a studio apartment, so it didn't take a lot of time to check.

"No, everything looks okay," Mia said. "Do you want a beer?"

"Sure."

Mia walked into her kitchen, pulled out a bottle of beer, and handed it to Sydney.

"I'm going to go take a shower and change real quick, okay?" Mia said.

"Okay," Sydney said, her expression flickering slightly.

Mia smiled. "Make yourself at home," she said, gesturing to the bed, basically the only place to sit in the apartment.

"Okay." Sydney opened the beer and took a drink.

Twenty minutes later, Mia emerged from her tiny bathroom and bit her lip when she saw that Sydney was asleep on her bed. She was lying at an angle; her feet, still in her shoes, were off the edge of the bed, like she hadn't wanted to get her shoes on the bed. Her phone was lying on the nightstand, and music was playing from it quietly, as if she couldn't be without some kind of noise. She lay half sitting up, her back against the pillows behind her, her head turned to the side.

Mia stared at Sydney in fascination. She was so cute with her bashfulness, but then so sexy with her gallant streak and her fast car. And then there was her edgy tomboy style and the fact that she'd come to Mia's rescue, even when Todd was much larger than Sydney. It tugged at Mia's heart that this young woman had rescued her, had stood up for her, this complete stranger. She knew that Sydney could have easily ignored what was going on; they hadn't even known she was out there. Sydney could have walked away with no one any the wiser, but she hadn't—she'd put herself in danger by confronting Todd. Who did that?

Mia walked over to the side of the bed where Sydney's feet were. She carefully untied and loosened the laces on the high-tops Sydney wore. She took the shoes off and set them aside. Then she walked around to the other side of the bed and climbed onto it carefully, trying not to disturb Sydney. She lay down on the bed, next to Sydney, her head on the pillow next to where Sydney's was turned. She stared at Sydney's face for a long while, finally getting sleepy herself. She fell asleep facing Sydney.

McKenna was tense on the drive home from the Body Shop. She'd discovered earlier in the evening that she didn't like to watch Cody riding her motorcycle. It was easy to see how many people paid no attention to motorcyclists. She saw how often people almost pulled into her and how closely others followed her.

"Does she have to push it like that?" McKenna asked from the back seat of Dakota's Ferrari.

Dakota grinned. "You should see her ride when she's pissed."

"No, thank you," McKenna said, doing her best to sit back and stop watching.

As it was, she'd kept an eye on how much Cody drank that night; fortunately it wasn't much. Cody took lithium for bipolar depression, and any drinking was inadvisable, but Cody could handle a certain amount without badly unbalancing her moods.

"Not too fast, Code, not too fast…" Dakota muttered.

"What?" McKenna asked, sitting up again.

Just as she did, there was a squealing of tires. The car in front of Cody's bike went into a spin, and Cody was too close to stop in time.

"Oh God!" McKenna screamed, as she saw Cody's bike go down and Cody slide clear of it.

"Fuck, hold on!" Dakota yelled, veering to turn her car to the side so she could protect Cody from being hit by any other drivers— they'd have to go through Dakota's Ferrari first.

Dakota was out of the car in a flash, heedless of any danger to herself, even as she shouted at Jazmine and McKenna to stay in the car and call 911. She didn't want either of them hit, or to see Cody if it wasn't good. Dakota slid to her knees, trying to assess Cody.

"Son of a bitch!" Jet said as she saw the accident, pulling her car up to further box in where Cody lay. Skyler pulled up on the back end of Dakota's car. The last thing they were going to allow was for someone to hit Cody.

Jet jumped out of her car, making sure it was clear for her to get Fadiyah out. She didn't want to put her wife in danger, but Fadiyah's nursing training would be useful at that point.

"Dakota, wait!" Jet shouted. Dakota was moving to take Cody's helmet off.

Dakota's head snapped around to look at Jet, then she nodded, seeing that Jet was bringing Fadiyah over to Cody.

"Cody, can you hear me?" Dakota was yelling.

There was no response. Fadiyah kneeled next to Cody and checked for a pulse.

"She has a pulse, Dakota. She's alive; she may just be unconscious," Fadiyah said, touching Dakota's sleeve.

"Is she okay?" McKenna asked as she walked over to them.

"Kenna, you needed to stay in the car," Dakota said.

"I need to see her," McKenna said.

They could hear sirens. Cody started to move her head.

"Do not move, Cody!" Fadiyah said loudly. "Just lie still, help is on the way. You will be okay."

McKenna kneeled next to Cody, touching her gloved hand.

"It's okay, babe. We're right here. Just lie still."

Cody seemed to relax then.

Half an hour later, the rest of the Lost Bois and their girls stood in the waiting room of the hospital, waiting to hear how Cody was. Harley texted Sydney to let her know what had happened. When the doctor finally came out, she talked to Dakota and McKenna as Cody's family.

"Miss Falco is resting comfortably. She has a concussion and some scrapes, but she will be fine."

A cheer went up from the small group in the waiting room.

McKenna walked into the hospital room to see Cody half sitting up on the bed, her eyes closed. McKenna walked around the bed and kissed Cody's forehead. Cody's hazel eyes opened immediately, and she smiled softly.

"You scared me," McKenna told her.

"I'm sorry," Cody said. "I could see something was going on in the car, and I was trying to catch up to see if it was anything I needed to intervene in. Then the car spun... I let the bike go so I wouldn't get under it. I'm sorry, babe..."

"The police were talking to the occupant of the car when we left with the ambulance," McKenna said. "They'll figure out what was wrong."

Cody nodded, looking relieved.

"Code?" Dakota queried from the foot of the bed.

"I'm okay, Kota," Cody told her.

Dakota walked over to the left side of the bed and climbed onto it, putting her head next to Cody's hip, her hand on Cody's stomach. Cody smiled at the gesture. Legally, Dakota was her sister; she was also her very best friend.

Cody put her hand on Dakota's head and stroked her hair, knowing that Dakota would have been as terrified as McKenna had been. McKenna sat on the bed on Cody's right side, putting her head above Cody's on the pillow, her hand stroking Cody's hair. Cody turned her face to her wife's, closing her eyes.

Lyric and Savanna strode into the hospital and were told where their daughter was and that their other two daughters were in with Cody. Lyric saw Jazmine standing with the rest of the group. She knew that the hospital wouldn't have let Jazmine in to see Cody, since Dakota and she weren't married. Walking over, Lyric took Jazmine's hand and led her with them to see Cody.

In the room, the three of them stood smiling as they saw Cody, McKenna and Dakota lying as they were on the bed. All three of them were asleep.

"Our girls," Savanna said softly to Lyric, winking at Jazmine, who smiled fondly.

Chapter 4

Mia woke first the next morning, used to her odd hours and not needing much sleep. She sat up carefully, not wanting to wake Sydney. She was surprised to see that Sydney had shifted during the night, and she must have gotten hot, because the lower half of her tank top was folded up over itself, exposing a fair amount of skin and nicely toned abs. Looking more closely, Mia could see that Sydney's arms were fairly toned as well, so she must work out. Mia found herself very tempted to touch those abs and arms.

She managed to control herself, although she found it took a lot of effort. What she did take the time to do was examine the necklace Sydney wore. It was a cross suspended on a black leather cord. It wasn't a Christian cross, because it was angled almost like a sword, with a sharply pointed cross inlaid in it. Mia was really curious about it; she touched the metal. That had Sydney stirring and opening her eyes, which seemed an even lighter gold in the morning light.

Sydney was very surprised to be looking at Mia. She smiled.

"Good morning," she said.

"Good morning," Mia said, smiling back. "What is this?" She held up the cross.

Sydney looked down at the cross in Mia's hand. "It's a Psi sword with a Southern Cross. It signifies the powers of the mind."

"Kind of a programmer thing?" Mia asked.

Sydney nodded, then she winced as her head ached.

"Uh-oh," Mia said. "Hungover?"

"A little bit."

"The way they were feeding you shots last night, it's no wonder."

"Well, it was my birthday," Sydney said, grinning.

"It was?" Mia asked.

"Yeah."

"And all I got you was nice big bruise on your cheek and a cut." Mia grimaced as she touched Sydney's cheek gently.

"No, you gave me a really great lap dance too," Sydney said.

"Your friend Jet gave me a hundred-dollar bill to make it a great first dance, you know."

Sydney tilted her head, blinking. "She did?"

Mia nodded.

"Is that why…" Sydney started to ask.

Mia shook her head. "I gave it back to her on the way out of the club last night. I think I enjoyed our dance as much as you did."

Sydney looked back at Mia, very obviously surprised. Mia moved forward, gazing into Sydney's eyes.

"I really wanted to kiss you last night," she said softly, her blue eyes searching Sydney's.

Sydney reached her hand up to Mia's cheek, moving her fingers to Mia's jawline and using her fingertips to bring Mia's face to hers. She kissed Mia's lips, then pulled back to look at her. Mia shifted forward and kissed Sydney, her kiss hungry and seeking.

Sydney's hands slid around Mia's waist, pulling her to her. Mia straddled her lap as their lips met over and over again. Mia was wearing the thinnest cotton shorts and a tank top, and she could feel her body pressing against Sydney's jeans. As Sydney began to move her hips, Mia moaned loudly, matching Sydney's rhythm. Mia found that she was getting more and more excited—she grasped at Sydney's shoulders, and her body heated up far more than the night before during the lap dance, but she knew that it was because this time Sydney was reciprocating the movement. She felt Sydney's hands on her hips, holding them, guiding them on her body.

"Oh my God," Mia moaned loudly, an orgasm overtaking her so strongly she had to hold on to Sydney's shoulders to keep from losing her balance as her body shook heavily, wracked by something akin to convulsions.

When the orgasm eased, she felt it begin to spiral upward once again. Sydney's movements pressed her closer, and Mia could feel her own wetness and desperately wanted to be closer to Sydney. She reached between them to unbutton Sydney's jeans, but she was stilled by Sydney's hands sliding up her waist, her fingers brushing over hard nipples. Once again Mia was screaming in orgasm, pressing her body against Sydney's desperately.

As her pulse eased, she lay against Sydney's body, feeling Sydney's hands on her back, in her hair. She reached down, unbuttoning Sydney's jeans and taking them off. Sydney watched her every movement with her gold, almost glowing eyes. Mia moved back up Sydney's body, kissing her as she came to lie on her side next to Sydney.

"I want to excite you," Mia said.

"You excite me," Sydney said, her voice husky, which served to arouse Mia more.

"I want to make you come," Mia said, her voice so shaky with desire Sydney moaned out loud.

Mia's hand on Sydney's stomach stroked the skin there. Sydney reached down and brought Mia's hand up to touch her very hard nipple. Mia moaned at feeling it, knowing that she was indeed exciting Sydney. Moving her fingers over the hard nub, Mia felt Sydney shudder, moaning softly again.

"Tell me how to make you come," Mia said, looking up at Sydney.

"Touch me," Sydney said, her voice so heated Mia could almost feel it.

Sliding her hand into the boy shorts that Sydney wore, Mia slipped her middle finger between the lips of Sydney's pussy and felt the heat and wetness there. Sydney's gasp and her body's upward jolt let Mia know she'd hit the right spot.

"I want to be inside you. Do you… can I…?" Mia asked.

"You can do anything to me…" Sydney said, pressing her body up toward her hand.

Mia slid her finger inside Sydney, and Sydney immediately began to come against Mia's hand. Mia felt her own body respond to Sydney's outcry; she came again along with Sydney.

Mia leaned her head against Sydney's shoulder as she sought to catch her breath.

"That was…" Mia began, trying to think of the right way to describe how she felt. Finally she shook her head, unable to come up with adequate words.

Sydney kissed Mia on the forehead, nuzzling her hair with her lips. Mia sighed, her body still tingling from the excitement she'd just been brought to. They lay together quietly for a few minutes. The silence was broken by Sydney's phone vibrating repeatedly; she reached for it and saw that it was Harley calling.

"Hey, Harley," she said.

"Where have you been? I've been texting you since last night!" Harley said.

"Damn, sorry," Sydney said, wincing at the tone of Harley's voice. "I fell asleep and my phone was on silent. What's going on?"

"Cody got into an accident last night," Harley said.

"Shit, what happened?" Sydney asked, shifting to sit up.

"Car in front of her spun out; she laid her bike down," Harley said gravely.

"Jesus, is she okay?" Sydney reached for her jeans, glancing at Mia, who was now sitting up and looking at her in concern.

"Yeah, she's got a concussion and some scrapes, but they said she'll be okay," Harley said. "We're all headed back to the hospital this morning at ten. Can you make it?"

Sydney glanced at the clock on the nightstand; it was 8 a.m.

"Yeah, I can get there. I gotta run home and change."

"Change?" Harley said, and Sydney could hear the grin in her voice.

Sydney closed her eyes and shook her head, looking extremely embarrassed.

"Don't start…" Sydney said to Harley.

"Oh, we're gonna talk," Harley said, laughing. "We'll see you in a bit."

"Okay, see you then. Bye."

"Bye."

Sydney hung up the phone, sliding it into to pocket of her jeans and buttoning them as she looked at Mia.

"What happened?" Mia asked.

"One of the girls got into an accident last night on the way home," Sydney said, sitting down to put on her shoes.

"Is she okay?" Mia asked, her eyes wide.

"Yeah, it sounds like it, but we're all meeting up at the hospital this morning to see her."

Mia nodded, looking a bit crestfallen.

Sydney saw the disappointed expression on her face. She turned, putting her hand to Mia's cheek.

"What is it?" she asked softly.

Mia shrugged. "I was…" She shook her head, looking away.

Sydney looked at her for a long moment. "Would you want to come with me to the hospital?"

Mia looked back at Sydney. "Do you think it would be okay?" she asked, not wanting to intrude.

"Of course," Sydney said, nodding.

"You said you need to go home and change. Where do you live?" Mia asked.

"West Hollywood."

Mia's eyes widened; West Hollywood was expensive.

"I can wait for you to get ready," Sydney said.

"Okay," Mia said. "I'll go take a quick shower."

"I'm gonna go smoke."

"Okay," Mia said, smiling.

A half hour later, Sydney walked back to the apartment. When Mia answered the door, Sydney was reaching up to pull her headphones out of her ears. Mia could still hear the music blaring from them before Sydney pulled the headphone jack out.

"Those look like some serious headphones," Mia noted, noting the various controls and the brand name Bose on the headphones.

"These headphones are my favorites," Sydney said, grinning as she held up the cups she was carrying.

She had found a Starbucks, where she'd gotten herself a dark espresso roast coffee and had guessed at what Mia would drink, getting her a chai tea.

"How did you know?" Mia asked.

"Guessed."

"You guessed perfect," Mia said, grinning.

"Good." Sydney smiled. "You look great."

Mia was dressed in jeans and a light-blue silky tank top with strappy sandals. Her hair was pulled back at the top into two long braids. Her makeup was light but served to enhance her already beautiful face.

Sydney couldn't resist touching that face.

"You are so beautiful," Sydney breathed, staring down into Mia's eyes, her expression reflecting simple amazement.

Mia smiled, her eyes lighting up at the words. She stepped closer to Sydney, nuzzling her lips against Sydney's neck as Sydney's arms wrapped around her. They stood that way for a long minute. Mia found that she really loved the feeling of Sydney's arms around her.

When they parted, Sydney looked down at Mia and kissed her gently. When she started to pull back, Mia put her hand behind Sydney's neck, deepening the kiss.

Sydney moaned against Mia's lips, her hands on Mia's back grasping and gathering her nearer. Mia wrapped her arms around Sydney's neck, pressing her body closer.

"Jesus…" Sydney murmured, her voice husky with desire.

Mia bit her lip, surprised by the feeling that gave her.

"I love that I excite you," Mia whispered.

"You do excite me," Sydney said, her mouth next to Mia's ear. "And believe me, I'd love to stay here…"

"I know," Mia said. "We need to get going."

"Yeah," Sydney said, grinning.

"Let's go," Mia said, grinning too. "Before I attack you and we're late."

Sydney chuckled, stepping back out of the embrace but holding her hand out. Mia took it, and they left the apartment.

In the car, Mia looked at Sydney, seeing once again how at ease she was behind the wheel of her car.

"Which one is Cody?" Mia asked, realizing she didn't remember. "I mean, I know she's one of the ones with DOJ, but which one was she?"

Sydney smiled. "I know it was probably a lot to take in last night, especially in the state you were in, so I understand. Cody was the one with short blond hair, one of the ones that was pointing a gun at your friend, Todd."

"Ex," Mia said. "Todd is my ex."

Sydney glanced over at her. "Can you tell me about that?" she asked gently. "Why he attacked you like that?"

Mia took a deep breath, surprised it had taken Sydney this long to ask about Todd.

"I only dated him for a month," Mia said, "and I guess he decided that he deserved what he didn't get while he was dating me."

Sydney's look was wary. "Why would he think he deserved anything?"

Mia studied Sydney for a moment. "I take it you've never dated men."

"Uh, no." Sydney looked a bit sickened by the thought, making Mia smile.

"Well, I can tell you that men think that if they're with you exclusively, it means you're going to put out," Mia said. "Don't lesbians think that way?"

"I can't speak for all lesbians," Sydney said, "but I don't think I 'deserve' anything. I mean, obviously you want that with someone you're dating, but I've dated someone for three months before we ever actually had sex. And I'd never even consider taking what I wanted forcibly. I wouldn't push the issue. If it wasn't happening, I'd figure it was at least half me, something I wasn't doing right." She shrugged. "Or maybe the chemistry just wasn't right."

Mia smiled. "I guess our chemistry was okay, huh?"

Sydney grinned. "Yeah, I think we might have some fairly amazing chemistry."

"I'm sure you have that a lot," Mia said, thinking that Sydney just had a way that was highly attractive.

Sydney looked at her in surprise. "No. Not like that."

"Really?" Mia asked, surprised too.

"I'm not saying I've never had good sex, but… not usually that quickly."

"Well, we did have a rather, um, odd introduction," Mia said, smiling.

"You mean the lap dance or the altercation?"

"Both," Mia said, rolling her eyes at the ludicrousness of the night before.

"It would definitely make an interesting 'how I met your mother' story," Sydney said with a grin.

Mia laughed. "I like that," she said, thinking she was already getting far too deep into this woman.

Sydney gave her a searching look. "Can I ask you a question?"

"Of course."

"Obviously you date men… at least you have… but… are you… I mean, are you bi?"

"Well, you are the first woman I've ever slept with," Mia said, "so I'm not sure what that makes me."

Sydney looked at her in complete shock.

"That was your first time?" Sydney asked, her voice as surprised as her look.

Mia nodded.

"Wow," Sydney said. "I had no idea…"

"Well, there's a bit more to it than that," Mia said tentatively.

"Will you tell me?" Sydney asked gently, noticing Mia's hesitation.

"I moved here from Oregon," Mia said, "right after I graduated high school. I'd met this guy on the internet, and he'd come to Oregon to meet me. He told me he loved me and that we'd be together. And we were. Things were okay until I got pregnant…"

"What happened?" Sydney asked.

"He broke up with me and kicked me out of the apartment," Mia said, looking sad. "I had to quit college so I could get a job. That's how I ended up at the Body Shop, and one of the girls told me I needed to get an abortion. In the end it didn't matter."

"What do you mean?" Sydney asked, concerned.

"They said that the fetus 'didn't thrive,'" Mia said sadly, "and I needed to get that procedure that they do to, like, clean everything out… after…"

"A D&C," Sydney said softly. "I helped a friend through a miscarriage before."

Mia blinked a couple of times, nodding.

"I couldn't afford to have it done at the time. I was already in so much debt for the medical appointments and stuff before that… so one of the girls took me down to TJ."

"Oh God…" Sydney murmured, grimacing.

"Yeah, I had no idea how… backwater that place was, but by the time we got there, I just wanted it done—I was in a lot of pain and sick as a dog. Anyway, whatever the guy did, he did something wrong… because the next time I tried to have sex with a man, it hurt so much I couldn't do it. It's never gotten better."

Sydney looked pained. "I'm sorry. That sucks."

Mia shrugged. "The girl who took me down is a lesbian. She and I would talk about what was going on with sex—she jokingly told me

I should just change teams, because lots of lesbians don't like penetration, so I'd fit right in."

Sydney wrinkled her nose at the assertion but understood what she was saying.

"Which was why you asked me…" Sydney said.

"Yeah," Mia said, biting her lip. "I knew she'd been joking, but it did get me thinking about the possibility…"

"Okay," Sydney said in a leading tone. "So I was kind of an experiment?" She didn't sound too offended by the idea.

"Well, I've been kind of checking out the women that come into the club, and no one even remotely attracted me until I saw you last night."

A smirk tugged at Sydney's mouth. Mia saw it and smiled.

"And then when I heard I had a lap dance and saw it was you…" Mia shook her head slowly. "I thought, well, this is my chance to test the attraction."

"Oh, you definitely tested it," Sydney said, grinning. "And my self control."

"You were extremely controlled," Mia said. "Way better than any man I've ever done that for."

Sydney moved her head around, stretching her neck, then looked over at Mia.

"Obviously I found you even more attractive after that," Mia said with a grin.

"Yeah?"

"Oh my God, so much. I had to get you out of that room, or I'd have risked my job by attacking you."

Sydney pressed her lips together. "Why do you think I was out in the back smoking?"

"Why?"

"Because a helluva a lot of cold water didn't work," Sydney said, waggling her eyebrows at Mia.

"Oh…" Mia said, smiling brightly. "Well, it was a good thing you were out there."

"Seems like."

"I couldn't believe the way you went after him." Mia shook her head. "I couldn't have imagined anyone ever doing something like that for me. And you were holding your own, too."

Sydney grinned. "I've been taking lessons from a retired MMA fighter."

"Oh, well, no wonder," Mia said, laughing.

When they got to Sydney's apartment, Mia was surprised by how nice the building was. It was far from the average apartment building. It was called The Crescent, and the lobby area and the pool that she could see as they walked through the lobby reminded Mia of a luxury hotel, not an apartment complex.

Inside the apartment, the first thing that Mia noticed was that the floors were all hardwood, and the kitchen had granite countertops, not the crappy chipped tile her apartment had.

Sydney glanced back at Mia and grinned. "Come on in," she said, seeing that Mia had stopped just inside the doorway and was staring openmouthed at the kitchen to the right.

"Wow, this place is…" Mia said, her eyes wide. "Wow."

Sydney laughed. "Come on," she said, taking Mia's hand and tugging her into the apartment.

Mia continued to gaze around, walking into the living room, seeing the marble corner fireplace and the small terrace outside. There was a painting on the wall behind the dark-brown leather couch. It looked like a black-and-white photograph of a railroad crossing, but there were streaks of yellow and green along the tracks.

"Is that a painting or a photo?" Mia asked, unable to tell, because it was definitely on a canvas.

"It's both actually," Sydney said. "The artist is Pete Kasprzak. He takes photos and then enhances them with paint strokes. I have three of his pieces. I really like his stuff; he reflects energy and life."

Mia smiled, pleasantly surprised by this information and the fact that Sydney was into art and photography.

"I want to study photography," Mia said. "I've been taking pictures since I was a kid. I love it."

"Well, you should do that," Sydney said. "College lets you explore things you love, and sometimes, if you're lucky, gives you a career too."

"Did you go to college for what you do?" Mia asked.

"Oh yeah," Sydney said. "And I have the student loans to prove it."

"What level of degree do you have?"

"I have a master's in computer science."

"Wow, so not just a regular degree," Mia said, impressed.

Sydney shrugged. "Computers was all I ever wanted to do, so I knew I needed to put in the work to get there."

"Does working for the state pay well?"

"Not too bad. The benefits are good, but I don't plan on staying with the state forever, just for ten years."

"Just ten years? Why ten years?" Mia asked.

Sydney grinned. "Because if I work for the state for ten years, they'll forgive my student loans."

"Is that a lot?"

"Well, I'm at about 120K, so…" Sydney said, rolling her eyes heavenward.

"Holy crap, what school did you go to?" Mia asked.

"Stanford," Sydney said. "They have one of the best computer science programs around," she explained at Mia's shocked expression.

"Uh-huh," Mia said with a grin and a pointed look, seeing that Sydney was trying to downplay her incredible education.

"Hey, Harley has a doctorate from MIT," Sydney said in her own defense.

Mia laughed. "That's why she's your boss."

"That, and she's worked for every law enforcement agency in the federal government. Okay, I'm going to go shower. Feel free to look around, make yourself at home."

"Okay," Mia said, smiling.

The first thing Mia heard was music coming from the bedroom; she heard the shower start shortly thereafter. She'd noticed that Sydney had music on a lot of the time. She also remembered the Bose headphones Sydney had back at the apartment. Mia had noticed no less than two Bose docking stations, in the office and in the living room. She assumed Sydney had one in her bedroom as well. The woman took her music seriously.

As Mia wandered around the apartment, she saw that Sydney had good taste in things and that she wasn't overly into decorating. She had a few pictures on the walls. Mia found both of the pieces Sydney had of Pete Kasprzak's. They were both black-and-white photos with the same strokes of color. One was a distance shot of the Las Vegas Strip, with the Mirage in the foreground and shafts of orange and yellow extending vertically from the area of the Strip itself. The other featured Mel's Drive-In, with streaks that started out yellow and red and phased to blue.

It was a two-bedroom apartment; the second bedroom was an office. Mia noticed that the computer with a really large monitor looked pretty hi-tech. It had a small alien-looking head on it with glowing green eyes, and the monitor had the same symbol. The poster on the wall above the computer said "Alienware," with heads of aliens in various colors.

Mia was out on the small terrace when Sydney emerged from her bedroom. Sydney walked out onto the terrace, standing behind Mia and leaning down to kiss her shoulder.

"You smell good." Mia said, catching a whiff of whatever cologne Sydney was wearing.

"Thanks," Sydney said, smiling. "You check everything out?"

"Yep, I figured out that you have a major thing for music, and what looks like a fairly expensive computer."

Sydney laughed. "I am very major into music, that's true—it keeps the ADD at bay. And if you're a programmer, you better have a serious computer. Alienware is one of the best."

"I see," Mia said, turning around.

Sydney was dressed in black skinny jeans, a black V-neck T-shirt, and burgundy combat boots that came up over the bottom of the jeans. The girl definitely had style.

Mia canted her head to the side. "ADD? You have attention deficit disorder?"

"Yeah."

"How does that work?"

Sydney turned to lean against the railing as she pulled out a cigarette and her lighter.

"Well, it just means that my brain is always jumping from one thing to the next in rapid succession."

"Do you take medication for it?" Mia asked.

"Nah," Sydney said. "I don't really need it. I know enough about my monster to keep it at bay."

Mia looked surprised by the term. "Your monster?"

Sydney took a drag on her cigarette. "Yeah, sometimes it's a monster, other times it's a two-year-old hyped up on sugar."

Mia widened her eyes slightly. "That's an interesting way to describe it."

Sydney shrugged. "It's how I see it."

"But doesn't it make it hard to do your job?"

"No," Sydney said. "Programming actually calms me down, and I'm able to focus on it. It's in a constant state of change; it's what I thrive on. It's why I crafted a career around it."

Once again, Mia was astounded by Sydney's obvious maturity and clarity of self.

"How old are you exactly?" Mia asked.

"Twenty-four as of yesterday," Sydney said, stubbing out her cigarette. "You?"

"Twenty," Mia said.

Sydney tilted her head to the side. "Don't you have to be twenty-one to work at the club?"

Mia grinned. "Ever heard of a fake ID?" she asked brightly.

"Oh, you're one of those bad girls I've heard about…"

"Yes, yes I am," Mia said, laughing.

Later that morning, they arrived at the hospital to see Cody. Naturally, Sydney was on the receiving end of a great deal of good-natured ribbing. Mia noted that Sydney took all of their comments with a grin and a shake of her head, but she didn't reply to any of them.

"Musta been one helluva lap dance," Jet said, giving a low whistle.

"The one she gave me was better," Mia said, winking at Jet.

That was greeted with a series of "OHs!" Jet's openmouthed shock was a much-lauded accomplishment. It also had Sydney laughing and hugging Mia to her.

"I like her," Quinn said, seeing that Mia had effectively shut Jet up for a moment.

***

"Jocelyn?" Sable called as she walked into the bathroom.

"Yeah?" Jocelyn answered from the shower, her voice barely audible.

Sable peeked into the shower and saw that Jocelyn was leaning her head against the tile wall, one hand on the wall next to her face. She was breathing heavily. Moving to the other side of the curtain, Sable was able to see Jocelyn's face—her eyes were closed, her lips pursing.

"Feeling sick again?" Sable asked gently.

Jocelyn nodded, her eyes still closed. Sable could see that Jocelyn still had soap on her body and in her hair. Sable took off her clothes and climbed into the shower behind Jocelyn.

"What are you doing?" Jocelyn asked, humor in her voice. "I'm so not in the mood right now…" She grinned.

Sable chuckled. "Damn," she said, smoothing her hand over Jocelyn's back. "Thought I'd help you out here."

Sable took the handheld shower head and used it to rinse Jocelyn's body off.

"Just hold on to me if you need to, babe," Sable said, feeling Jocelyn's body waver as Sable touched her back and moved in front of her.

Jocelyn put one hand on Sable's shoulder, but Sable could tell she wasn't putting her full weight on her. The woman was still a gentleman even when she was as sick as a dog from her first round of chemotherapy. She could feel Jocelyn shaking and knew she needed to get

102

her out of the shower soon. The fatigue was really beating her down, and Sable was worried about her going back to work the next day. They'd extended their "vacation" to give Jocelyn time to get through the worst of the chemo side effects. Unfortunately, the fatigue, nausea and nasty bruising from the IV were holding on even after a week.

"Babe, I need to rinse your hair, but you need to sit down, okay?" Sable said.

Jocelyn nodded and sat on the bench in the shower stall; Sable helped her. The last thing they needed right now was another bruise or, God forbid, a broken bone. Jocelyn groaned as she sat down, doubling over as another wave of nausea hit her. She retched, dry heaving, because there was nothing in her stomach to throw up anymore. Sable did her best to soothe her, using the acupressure technique Jocelyn had told her Gage used with her migraines. Fortunately, the cancer had somehow abated the migraines for the most part; it would be a cruel joke to be sick from chemo and have a mind-splitting headache at the same time.

"I've got some stuff I want to try when you get out of the shower, for the nausea," Sable said as Jocelyn sat back up, leaning back against the wall of the shower.

"Like what?" Jocelyn said, raising an eyebrow.

"Some stuff I got from Fin. She said Kai swears by it."

"She told Kai?" Jocelyn asked sharply.

"No, babe," Sable said. "She looked in the books that Kai has for all her essential oil stuff and found the recipes. I told you she promised me that she wouldn't tell Kai."

Jocelyn nodded, looking tired. Sable had told Jocelyn about seeing Finley at the hospital and that Finley had promised to keep Jocelyn's cancer a secret, even from her fiancée.

Twenty minutes later, Sable had helped Jocelyn out of the shower and into a warm bathrobe, having her sit in a chair while she dried her hair. So far they'd gotten lucky in that area—Jocelyn's hair remained thick and intact. They hadn't been sure how they'd hide hair loss.

Sable had a diffuser going in the room, with the scents of lavender, peppermint and ginger in it. It was the same mixture she massaged into Jocelyn's stomach a little while later.

"The doctor doesn't want us to use those anti-nausea pills too often," Sable told her as she massaged Jocelyn's abdomen gently. "He says they lose effectiveness if you use them too much. So I figure you can use them at work... Are you sure you should go back yet, babe?" she asked, glancing at the almost black bruises on the inside of Jocelyn's arms and the nasty one she'd gotten on her hip from running into the dresser in the middle of the night as she ran to the bathroom to throw up.

"There's wildfires springing up already and it's early in the season," Jocelyn said, her voice soft. "Gage'll be losing her shit if we're not ready. She needs me."

Sable breathed in deeply, wanting to argue with Jocelyn again about needing to tell Gage the truth about the cancer. She knew that Gage would force Jocelyn to take care of herself and not worry about the office. Unfortunately, Sable knew that if she told Gage, Jocelyn would likely never forgive her, and she couldn't take that chance either, not unless she had no choice. If Jocelyn didn't fare well going into the office, Sable would have to reconsider violating Jocelyn's trust. Her health was much more important than worrying about how the cancer would affect Gage.

***

In the office the next day, Gage noted that Jocelyn was wearing long sleeves, even though it was the beginning of summer in Los Angeles and already getting hot. Later that day, she started getting reports from people that they'd heard Jocelyn throwing up in the bathroom. She talked to Kit about her concerns that night.

"What do you think is going on?" Kit asked Gage.

They were lying in bed, wearing light pajamas since Caitlyn was at the house that night. Kit's mother continually offered to take Caitlyn so Kit and Gage could have "adult time." Gage found it endlessly amusing, whereas Kit was mortified.

"I'm not sure," Gage hedged, "but I'm worried it's drugs. I know Sable's been known to use."

"But why would Gun be throwing up?"

"Sometimes if you take too much, it happens. And she's wearing long sleeves in summer?" She shook her head. "Gun is all about tank tops in the summer. I think she's hiding something."

Kit grimaced. "You really think she's getting into drugs though?"

Gage shook her head again. "I really hope not."

"Okay, but if she is, what will you do?" Kit asked.

"I'd have to force her into rehab, and I'd need to get Sable away from her."

"You think you could do that?" Kit asked, shocked.

"I think I'd damned well try, Hell, I'd pull BJ Sparks in if I have to. He's got Sable's contract; he could make her life hard if he wanted to."

Kit chewed on her lip, looking worried.

"You might irreparably damage your relationship with Gun if you do that, you know," Kit pointed out, knowing Gage needed to hear it.

Gage pressed her lips together in consternation and in determination. "I love her, and if that's what I have to do to keep her from killing herself, that's what I'll do."

Kit nodded sadly. "I hate that this is happening with you two."

Gage smiled softly at her. "I'm glad you understand why I'm worried."

Kit looked surprised by the comment. "Why wouldn't I? She's your best friend."

"Yeah, but you thought she was more before, remember?"

"I know, but you told me how it is with you two, so now I understand."

Gage grinned. "Oh, babe, you have no idea …"

"What do you mean?" Kit asked, trying to understand what Gage was saying.

"I mean that other women I dated couldn't handle my relationship with Gun. They didn't get it and they didn't want to get it. What they wanted was for me to stop being friends with someone I was that close to."

"Because of the sex?" Kit knew that Jocelyn and Gage had been there for each other in every way, including sexually when needed.

"Oh yeah, and because Gun was the one I'd call when I needed help or to be talked down from something. They just couldn't handle it."

Kit looked back at her, then shrugged. "Then they didn't love you, at least not like I do. I trust you, Gage, and when you tell me you love me, I believe you."

Gage smiled, her eyes staring directly into Kit's. "And that's why I love you."

***

106

Jocelyn looked at Gage, her lips curled in a slight grin.

"Okay," she said mildly.

Gage had just introduced her to her assistant, a young man named Jack.

"Jack can help you with this transition to the new accounting and procurement system," Gage said. "He's worked in both areas."

Jocelyn surveyed Jack—he appeared to be in his early twenties. He had medium-brown hair, and bright blue eyes. He also looked like family.

When Gage walked out of her office, Jocelyn turned to Jack again.

"Who did you piss off?" she asked, raising an eyebrow at the man.

"No one, that I know of," Jack said, grinning. "But I'm sure that's going to change soon."

Jocelyn had to stifle a smile. "Why's that?"

"'Cause there were a couple of people vying for this job."

"People wanted to work for me?" Jocelyn asked, sounding stunned.

Jack tilted his head. "An executive deputy director who drives a Viper and is dating Sable Sands? In Los Angeles? Hell yeah!"

"Ah," Jocelyn said as she understood the sudden attraction to her. "So, give me the lowdown on what this new system is going to entail."

"Pure unadulterated hell," Jack said.

"Oh, I feel better already," Jocelyn said, rolling her eyes.

Two hours later she found herself in her car with Jack, on their way to a meeting with the transition team for the new system being set in place for all state agencies. Jack got a good preview of his new boss when she got into a vehicular dispute with another driver who cut her off.

"Nice," Jocelyn muttered, throwing her hands up at the other driver.

Suddenly, the other driver, a man in a lifted truck, slowed down and then slammed on his brakes.

"Fucker!" Jocelyn cussed, yanking the wheel of the Viper to zip around the man.

The truck moved into the lane she'd shifted into, and they could see that the man was hanging out his window, cussing at her.

"Are ya fuckin' kidding me right now?" Jocelyn growled, gunning the engine of the Viper. As it shot forward, she flipped the guy off and got around him before he could cut her off again, this time on purpose.

"Oh, and now you think you're gonna push up on me?" Jocelyn asked, glancing in her rearview mirror. "See if you can keep up, skippy!" she crowed as she downshifted and put her foot down on the gas pedal.

"Woooo!" Jack yelled, laughing as they went speeding down the freeway. "That was awesome!" he said ecstatically as Jocelyn slowed back down. The truck had been left in the dust easily.

Jocelyn glanced at him and could see the pure glee on his face. Maybe this kid wasn't so bad…

Two hours later, she walked out of the meeting, shaking her head.

"Well that's two hours of my life I'm never fucking getting back," Jocelyn muttered to Jack. "Should I even ask where we are with any of that shit they were talking about?"

Jack's expression was pointedly devoid of emotion.

"I'm taking that as a 'not very fucking far at all, Gun,'" Jocelyn said. "Jesus fucking Christ, was the other guy just as useless as the director?"

"Pretty much," Jack said. "Except that his assistant was male, and way too young to be here."

"Oh…" Jocelyn murmured, her eyes widening, then she looked at Jack. "Can I ask you something?"

"You're the boss, of course you can."

"Well, this isn't work related."

"Then yes, I'm gay," Jack said, grinning.

Jocelyn nodded, grinning too. "And that was what I was going to ask."

"Family all the way." Jack winked. "That's part of why I wanted to work for you."

"To catch a break from all the heterosexuality in the place?"

"You could say that," Jack said, his blue eyes twinkling. "So can I ask you a question?"

"Go for it," Jocelyn said as they climbed back into the Viper.

"Are the rumors about you and the director true?"

Jocelyn looked at him with a smirk. "Which ones?"

"Were you two in the military together?" Jack asked.

Jocelyn laughed. "Yeah, I was her gunner."

"Hence the name Gun?"

"Part of my middle name too."

"But the rumors about you two being a couple…" Jack glanced at her, wondering if he was over-stepping.

"We were, but it was a long time ago," Jocelyn said.

"So you two aren't fighting because of Sable Sands?"

"Not hardly," Jocelyn said, rolling her eyes. "She's with Kit."

"People are saying she really wants to be with you."

"Well, people are wrong. She's in love with Kit," Jocelyn said, her voice sharp in her need to defend Gage.

Jack nodded, looking surprised by her tone.

"Sorry," Jocelyn said.

"It's okay," Jack said.

"So people think you're fighting with Gage because of me?" Sable asked, surprised.

"Apparently," Jocelyn said, sounding annoyed. "I hope that shit doesn't work its way around to Kit…"

Sable made a noise in the back of her throat. "Yeah, or this will have all been for naught."

Jocelyn made a face, nodding.

Chapter 5

"Lyric, can I ask you a question?" Tyler queried, as she and Lyric worked on the Chevelle.

"Sure," Lyric said. "What's up?"

Tyler stood up, wiping her hands on a rag and reaching for the beer Savanna had brought out for her.

"When Savanna had Anna, did you two have any issues?" Tyler asked.

"Like what?"

Tyler blew her breath out. "Shen and I just can't seem to get... I don't know... back to good, you know?"

Lyric nodded. "Yeah, Vanna had some issues after she had Anna. She felt fat and ugly and all that."

Tyler looked relieved. "Okay, yeah, that right there. And no matter what I say, it's not right..."

Lyric rolled her eyes. "Oh, hell yeah. I thought she was going to take my head off a couple of times!"

"Exactly!" Tyler said. "So it's totally a new-mom thing..." Tyler grimaced. "'Course, Savanna probably didn't have some fucking kid fawning all over her, did she?"

"What kid?" Lyric asked.

"That Kimber who was Gun's thing and tried to get at Harley," Tyler said, her lips curling in irritation.

"Oh... what the hell is she doing near Shenin?"

"Gage made her Shen's assistant." Tyler's tone was mild, but the look on her face indicated her annoyance at that fact.

"What the fuck?" Lyric said, apparently mystified.

"Gage apologized, but it was all she had when Shen got back."

"Yeah, I don't fuckin' care. She should have figured something else out," Lyric said.

Tyler smiled, glad to have someone on her side.

"So is she hitting on Shenin?" Lyric asked suspiciously.

"Shen says she's not, but…" Tyler shook her head.

"You don't believe her."

"I think she's trying to keep the peace."

"You don't think Shenin's interested, do you?" Lyric asked.

Tyler shrugged. "I don't know. I mean, this is a kid… and it sounds like she's a bit of a freak…"

"So? Shenin loves you, Ty. She always has, from the sounds of it."

Tyler nodded. She'd spent a lot of time over the years wondering what Shenin was doing with her. Shenin hadn't been gay when they'd met, and it had been their close friendship that had turned into love, but Tyler had always been waiting for Shenin to figure out that she could have any woman on the planet she chose, and leave. Tyler had never been confident about her ability to hold on to women, and Shenin was by far the most incredible and most beautiful woman she'd ever been with. She always figured she was Shenin's "starter lesbian" and eventually she'd move on to something better.

Lyric could see that Tyler was really worried about Shenin. She had no idea what to say to Tyler to convince her that Shenin was in love with her. She'd known the couple for over three years, and she honestly felt like they were a good match. Tyler was the strong, easygoing, stable presence, and Shenin was the outgoing, slightly wild child, but her love for Tyler seemed to temper that.

Putting her hand on Tyler's shoulder, Lyric gave her a serious look. "Hang in there, Ty. She loves you—I'd bet my Ducati on it."

Tyler nodded, trying her best to take heart in Lyric's conviction.

It wasn't helping that Shenin was coming home later and later. She said that they were working overtime to gear up for the fire season, and fires had already started in some of the mountainous regions. In Tyler's mind, it was just an excuse to stay in the office with Kimber for longer periods of time. Worse still, Tyler and Shenin hadn't been intimate in almost a month, and even that encounter had been brief, rushed, and not fully satisfying for either of them. Tyler's imagination was working overtime.

***

"Mom, she likes me!" Colby told Kashena excitedly when she and Sierra walked in the door one afternoon.

"You finally got up the nerve to ask?" Kashena asked, grinning.

"Yeah," Colby said. "I guess I haven't lived around you long enough to inherit the playa genes."

"Oh lord," Sierra said, rolling her eyes. "I'm going to go change," she told Kashena, kissing her on the lips. "Will you start the coals?"

"Yep," Kashena said. "Come on, Col, let me teach you all about charcoal and the proper way to set it up."

"So how do I ask her out?" Colby asked as he studiously arranged coals.

"You just ask, Col," Kashena said. "You come up with a plan, like coffee or something, and you just say 'I'd like to take you for coffee' or 'Hey, have you seen *Rogue One* yet? I want to see it and I'd love for you to go with me.' But that's only if she's a Star Wars geek like you." She winked at him.

"She has a BB8 backpack," Colby said.

"A whosy-what?" Kashena asked.

"Star Wars geek stuff, Mom," Colby said, grinning.

Kashena smiled widely. "Well, there ya go, match made in... space."

"A what?" Sierra asked as she walked out onto their patio.

"The girl, she's a Star Wars geek, like your son," Kashena said.

"Oh, sure, he's my son when he likes space movies, but he's yours when he gets all As."

"Duh." Kashena grinned.

"So when are you going to ask her out?" Sierra asked, sitting down on the chaise longue.

"I don't know yet," Colby said, pensively, "but soon. How did Kash ask you out?"

Kashena and Sierra looked at each other. Kashena shrugged, shaking her head. It was her way of telling Sierra it was up to her what she wanted to tell Colby.

"She never really asked me out," Sierra said, her eyes on Kashena. "We'd known each other back in college... and then she became my bodyguard..."

"Yeah, I remember when she came to the house to pick you up," Colby said, then got an odd look on his face. "That was before Dad got back."

Sierra nodded and glanced at Kashena again; they were both waiting for Colby to make the connection. They could almost hear the click when understanding dawned.

"Were you two dating when Dad came back?"

Sierra took a deep breath. She knew it wasn't in Kashena to lie, and she found that she didn't want to lie to Colby either, even if it made them all a little uncomfortable.

"Yes," Sierra said to Colby. "Kashena and I had reconnected at that point, and things with your dad were tenuous at best. They only got worse when he came home from Iraq."

"But he'd been in a war…" Colby said. "Maybe it was just hard on him."

Kashena and Sierra looked at each other, each of them surprised that Colby was now trying to defend Jason, who'd almost killed Kashena in front of the two of them a couple of years before.

"Colby," Sierra began hesitantly, "things between your dad and me had never been great."

Colby cast his eyes down. "He was in a war, Mom. He deserved you to be faithful to him during that."

"Kashena was in a war too, Colby, and she never raped me when she didn't get what she wanted," Sierra snapped, her dark eyes flashing in anger.

Colby's head snapped up. Kashena put her hand out to Sierra, seeing that she wanted to say more, but Kashena knew that things were about to get bad really quick.

Sierra strode into the house. Kashena watched her go, knowing that she was taking herself out of the conversation to keep from blowing up at Colby again.

"Colby," Kashena said calmly, "I know you want to remember things your own way, but your father was abusive to your mother, verbally and physically. I can show you pictures from what he did to her if that will help. There was a reason he was in jail, Col. I'm sorry, but that's a fact."

"He raped Mom?" Colby asked tremulously.

"Yeah," Kashena said, "and he backhanded her right in front of you. That was the night you and your mother came to stay with me. Do you remember that?"

Colby nodded. "Kind of. I remember being surprised that you were a Marine too, like my dad." Colby sighed. "I guess something inside me worries that I'm like him. So I keep thinking if I can find something redeeming about him, then maybe I'm not that bad."

"Colby, you're not like your father," Kashena said. "You're so much like your mother it's not even funny. You're intelligent, caring, and becoming a good man right before our eyes."

Colby seemed near tears. He knew that Kashena was exactly the "male role model" that was making him into a good man.

"I'm sorry, Mom," he said. "I didn't mean to sound like a jerk."

"I know, Col," Kashena said, "but I'm not the one you need to apologize to." She glanced toward the house.

Colby nodded, looking contrite. "I don't know what to say…"

"Part of being a man is being able to apologize when you screw up." Kashena touched his shoulder. "Just tell her what's in your heart, Col. She loves you more than you'll ever know."

Colby nodded again. Turning, he walked into the house. Kashena watched him go. She knew this was part of growing up for Colby. She understood his fear of becoming like Jason; Kashena watched constantly for any sign of violence in Colby. She'd done her best to direct his energies toward constructive things like working out at the gym and running. She was considering having him start training with Kai and Remington, but she hadn't talked to Sierra about that yet. The way Kashena saw it, Kai and Remington were two of the best and most respectful women she knew, and if they couldn't instill that in Colby, no one could. Since they both had been Marines, it also would serve to show Colby two more Marines who would never consider getting violent with a woman no matter what.

Inside the house, Colby found Sierra sitting in the living room. He walked over to where she sat, kneeled on the floor in front of her, and took her hands in his, staring up at her.

"I'm sorry, Mom," he said, his eyes, so much like Sierra's, glazed with tears. "I didn't remember… I just don't want to be like him, so much that it scares me…"

Sierra gazed at her son, seeing Jason's coloring but her eyes, and her proud American Indian heritage in his high cheekbones and strong jawline.

"You will never be like him, Colby," Sierra said, sitting forward and looking directly into his eyes. "Kashena and I won't allow that to happen. Your father had a dreadful role model to learn from—your grandfather was a terrible man. But you have Kashena, and she's teaching you the things you need to know to be a good man. You don't need to make a hero out of your father to do that. Okay?"

"Okay," Colby said, doing his best to let his fears go.

Sierra smiled at him. "I love you, Colby."

"I love you too, Mom," he said, hugging her.

Kashena watched from the patio doors and smiled. Raising a boy wasn't an easy task.

***

Sydney woke with Mia in her arms. They'd been together almost constantly since they'd met just under a week ago. Amazingly, they seemed to click on a lot of things, and Sydney found that she was very comfortable in Mia's presence.

Looking down at the girl, she caught herself smiling yet again. Mia was so beautiful, with her pastel rainbow hair, blue eyes, and lashes that were almost white when she wasn't wearing makeup. Sydney touched Mia's face, always feeling the need to touch her to see if she was real. Mia stirred, moving her head then opening her eyes, and looked up at Sydney.

"Morning." Sydney smiled, her gold eyes soft.

"Hi," Mia said, smiling too.

Sydney kissed her softly.

"Mmm," Mia murmured against Sydney's lips, pressing her body closer.

Sydney slid her hands over Mia's skin, pulling her closer and deepening the kiss. Within minutes they were making love. Afterwards, Sydney lay over Mia, her arms holding most of her weight off the smaller girl.

"It's amazing that you can do that to me so easily," Mia said, staring up at Sydney in wonder.

Sydney smiled and shifted her weight so she could lie to Mia's side, keeping her hand on Mia's bare skin as she leaned in to kiss her temple.

"What time did you get here?" Sydney asked, having never even heard Mia come in.

"Around three," Mia said, "but I took a shower and everything before I came over."

Sydney nodded, appreciating that fact—the last thing she wanted to smell on the woman she was intimate with was a man. When Mia worked, Sydney did her best not to think about it.

"Did you have fun last night?" Mia asked, knowing that Sydney had gone to the Club with the Lost Bois and the rest of the group.

"Yeah," Sydney said. "It was fun. We drank, we watched the girls dance… same old thing."

"Why don't you dance with the girls?" Mia asked. "I saw how well you move…"

Sydney shrugged, her expression non-committal. "Most of the single girls there last night were either exes or straight girls looking for an adventure. I already have enough toaster ovens."

"Huh?" Mia seemed befuddled.

Sydney laughed. "Uh, it's a les thing—there's a joke that every time a gay woman turns a straight girl, she gets a toaster oven."

"I see," Mia said. "And I'm guessing I'm not the only toaster oven you've ever earned?"

Sydney's gold eyes sparkled as she shook her head.

"So, how many toaster ovens would you have?" Mia asked with a petulant look.

"I'm not sure I should answer that question."

"Tell me," Mia said, pushing Sydney onto her back and covering her body with her own.

"I, um… oh…" Sydney moaned as Mia slid her body down over hers.

"Tell me, or I stop," Mia said.

"Oh, God… Um… I don't… I can't think…" Sydney said, her hands on Mia's hips.

"You want me to stop?" Mia asked, pausing her movements.

"No!" Sydney exclaimed, making Mia smile. "I just… like… I don't… Six. I think six."

Mia paused, shocked. "Seriously?"

"Not fair. I told you…" Sydney flexed her hands on Mia's hips.

Mia kissed Sydney's lips and started moving her body again, pressing in all the right places. Before long Sydney was coming and Mia was as well.

Afterwards, Mia looked down at Sydney. "So six, huh?"

119

"I think so," Sydney said, grinning.

"So many that you lose count," Mia said, narrowing her eyes.

Sydney laughed, shaking her head. "I just…"

"I can see it," Mia said. "You're cute, you aren't really intimidating, and you're very sweet."

Sydney didn't reply, looking a bit embarrassed.

"So do you date them after? Or…" Mia asked, letting her voice trail off.

"Sometimes. It depends on the situation."

"So in what situations wouldn't you date them after?" Mia asked, curious now.

"Well, two of them were married."

"To men?"

"Yeah," Sydney said. "Hence the toaster…"

"Oh yeah, duh, sorry. So you wouldn't date them because they were married to men?"

"I don't date people who are married, gay or straight," Sydney said. "It's not right."

"Do all lesbians think that way?" Mia asked.

"Nope," Sydney said. "I'm not saying that all lesbians will date married people, but some of us think that if a woman is married to a man, then she's fair game."

"Really? Because men don't count?"

"Well, I can tell you that Jet figures if men can't do their jobs as men, and we lesbians can do what they can't, then we have the right, actually the duty, to do so."

"Whoa," Mia said. "That's… wow…"

Sydney laughed. "I know."

"So has she?"

"What? Dated a married woman?"

Mia nodded.

"You met Ashley, right?" Sydney asked.

"The one married to Sebastian?"

"Yeah."

"She's beautiful… but wait, you're saying that Jet dated her?" Mia asked.

Sydney nodded.

"Does Jet have a death wish?" Mia had seen Sebastian Bach and thought that he could make mincemeat out of Jet.

"Oh, wait." Sydney held up her hand. "This was before she met Sebastian. She was married before."

"Oh," Mia said, sounding relieved. "I was confused, 'cause he and Jet seemed like they got along pretty good."

"Yeah, they're pretty good friends."

Mia nodded. "But he's like best friends with Kashena, right? The one that's a director at your office?"

"Right."

"Yeah, she's cool," Mia said, smiling. "All ex-Marine and stuff…"

"Uh-huh." Sydney raised an eyebrow. "Sierra'd kill you."

Mia laughed, shaking her head. "I'm not crazy. I've got the butch I want to be around."

"Oh, you do?" Sydney asked, smiling.

"Uh-huh," Mia said.

They kissed for a few minutes, then Sydney shifted Mia to her side.

"So what's on our agenda for today?" Sydney asked, glancing at the clock; it was already 10:30 a.m.

"Well…" Mia said, looking hesitant. "I need to go to the makeup store. Would you be willing to go with me?"

"There's a makeup store?" Sydney asked, shocked.

"Yep," Mia said, smiling. "A whole store dedicated to all things makeup."

"That's kind of scary," Sydney said. "But sure, I'll brave it."

Mia smiled. "I couldn't get a man to go in there to save my life."

"Good thing I'm not a man, then."

"Mm-hmm…" Mia kissed Sydney again.

It amazed Mia how easy she found it being with Sydney. She never felt strange or out of place. When they were in public together and Sydney took her hand, it never even occurred to her that anyone would think it was strange. To Mia it seemed natural and far from weird. Every so often she'd see people glancing at them, the looks on their faces wary or derisive, and that was when it would occur to her that they were doing something that wasn't commonplace, and that it was probably something Sydney dealt with far more often. Sydney had a very definite butch look about her, and she would rarely be mistaken for anything but a lesbian. Whereas Mia would never be seen as gay unless she was holding hands with Sydney, Sydney would always be pegged as gay. She realized it was the vast difference between femmes and butches.

That afternoon, walking into Ulta, she saw people look over at them. People always looked at Mia because of her hair; she knew that always attracted attention. The girl at the front counter called a greeting to them, and Mia noticed that her eyes went from Mia to Sydney and stayed on Sydney for an extra-long moment. Mia glanced at Sydney to see if she noticed—she didn't, she was busy gazing at all the different makeup displays and counters. After a long minute, Sydney looked down at Mia, who grinned.

"Come on, before you overload," Mia said, taking Sydney's hand and leading her over to where the Urban Decay makeup was.

Sydney had a good time browsing through all the colors of the eyeshadows and lipsticks. Mia even showed her the various palettes that Urban Decay had, one of which was eyeshadow that sparkled.

"That's cool," Sydney said, her eyes wide.

Mia caught the eye of a woman walking past them; the woman seemed amused by Sydney's obvious enthusiasm. Mia laughed. It was hard to resist Sydney's childlike exuberance sometimes. She had a way about her that spoke of an innate innocence. Mia knew that Sydney was far from naive or foolish, but at times Sydney seemed completely open and easy, and it was a very charming aspect of her personality.

"What does this do?" Sydney picked up a tester of liquid eyeliner and unscrewed the cap, holding it up to look at the thin brush with a bright blue on it. "Oh, cool," she said, smiling, then touched the brush to the back of her hand. "Oh, you need to get this one," Sydney said. "It goes with your eyes... It's for eyes, right?"

"Yes," Mia said, smiling. "It's eyeliner," she said, pointing to the eyeliner she currently wore.

"Awww," Sydney said, nodding slowly. "Oh, this one's cool too... and this one... oh, and this... Okay you need all of those." She circled her finger to indicate all of the colors.

"Syd, that's like ten colors, and they're twenty-two dollars each."

Sydney looked back at her unfazed. "Okay." She picked up one of each of the colors.

Mia stared at her openmouthed. "That's like two hundred and twenty dollars."

"Oh, wait," Sydney said, picking up the palette that went with the colors and putting it into the basket Mia held.

"That's like fifty," Mia said, her tone rising in panic. "Syd, I don't have that kind of money."

"I do," Sydney said, smiling.

"No," Mia said.

"Yes," Sydney said, reaching over to take the basket out of Mia's hand. "What else did you need to get?"

Mia stared up at Sydney. "Are you crazy?"

"Sometimes." Sydney's gold eyes sparkled.

Mia gave her a pointed look. "Like right now?"

"Sounds like," Sydney said, a grin on her lips.

"Are you sure?"

Sydney smiled. "I'm sure."

Mia put her arm around Sydney's neck. "You don't have to," she said, looking up into Sydney's eyes.

"I know," Sydney said. "I want to."

"Thank you." Mia kissed her.

Someone cleared their throat behind them. Sydney, whose arm was around Mia's waist, just sidestepped, tugging Mia with her, keeping her lips on Mia's. Mia started laughing at the movement, glancing at the middle-aged woman passing them. The woman was throwing them a disgusted look.

"Don't like it, don't look," Mia snapped, then looked back up at Sydney, who simply quirked her lips in a grin.

Apparently that kind of thing didn't bother Sydney at all.

On the way out of the store, where Sydney had dropped just under three hundred dollars, Sydney glanced over at Mia.

"Are you hungry?" she asked. "I'm hungry."

Mia smiled. "Okay."

"Do you like sushi?"

"Um…" Mia looked worried.

"Okay, how about Greek?"

Mia wrinkled her nose up.

"Betting crawfish is out too…" Sydney said, grinning now.

"Ugh!" Mia said. "Mud bugs!"

Sydney laughed at that one. Then she gave Mia a stern look.

"Okay, it's either sushi or Greek—which is it?"

"But…"

"You need to try things, babe," Sydney said gently.

"Maybe I'm not really hungry…"

"Woman!" Sydney exclaimed. "You have got to trust me."

"Fine," Mia said, sighing. "Greek, I guess."

Sydney smiled. "Okay."

At the restaurant, Sydney turned to Mia. "Do you like anything like lamb? Or am I sticking to regular meat?"

Mia gave her a pointed look.

"Normal meat it is," Sydney said, grinning. "Okay, do you trust me?"

"I'm not sure," Mia said, staring at Sydney like she wasn't sure she knew her anymore.

Sydney laughed, then turned to the waitress who'd been waiting patiently to take their order.

"Okay, so two classics—one with gyros, the other with grilled chicken, and the tzatziki on the side for the grilled chicken. I want an order of spanakopita, and can you have them put in two orders of baklava?"

"You got it," the waitress said, smiling at Sydney. "Drinks?"

"Beer for me. Babe?" she asked Mia.

"Coke?" Mia said.

The waitress nodded, writing it down and looking at Sydney. "Got ID, cutie?"

Sydney reached into her back pocket for her wallet and handed her ID to the waitress with a smile, winking at Mia. The waitress nodded again, handing it back to Sydney.

"Thanks," she said with another smile and a wink of her own, then walked away, an exaggerated swing to her hips.

Sydney canted her head as she watched the girl walk away.

"Excuse me…" Mia said, looking sternly at Sydney.

"Huh?" Sydney murmured, seeing the look on Mia's face. A slow grin spread over her lips. "What?"

"What?" Mia mimicked sarcastically.

Sydney smiled. "Hey, just because I know what's for dinner, doesn't mean I can't look at the menu."

Mia opened her mouth in surprise, then shook her head. "You just can't keep them away, can you?"

"She's harmless," Sydney said. "A lot of them flirt; it's so they can get a good tip."

"Uh-huh," Mia murmured, narrowing her eyes suspiciously. "You can't even tell when they're serious, can you?"

Sydney looked at Mia, her mouth twitching.

A few minutes later, when the waitress brought Sydney's spanakopita, Mia looked at it and made a face.

"Have you ever tried anything different?" Sydney asked as she used her fork to cut into the pastry.

Mia grinned. "Yeah, I moved to Los Angeles from Bend, Oregon."

"I meant food-wise," Sydney said, taking a bite.

"Sure. I never knew what French fries tasted like till I tried them."

"When?"

"When I was two."

Sydney shook her head. "Will you try this?" she asked, indicating the spanakopita.

"Uh, no," Mia said.

"Do you even know what's in it?"

"Nope, but it looks… green." Mia wrinkled her nose again.

"Oh God, tell me you're not one of those people that won't eat certain colors of food."

"What's the green stuff?" Mia asked.

"Spinach."

"Uck," Mia said.

"Try it," Sydney said.

Mia shook her head. "Uh-uh."

"Babe…" Sydney said, giving Mia a sidelong look.

"Don't "babe" me," Mia said. "I don't like spinach. It's mushy."

"Mushy?"

Mia grinned. "Yeah."

Sydney shook her head and continued to eat until the small pastry was gone.

When their lunch came, Mia looked at the food suspiciously.

"I promise, it's completely spinach free," Sydney said.

All the same, Mia carefully checked out the contents of the plate.

"It's grilled chicken, lettuce, tomato, cucumber and pita," Sydney told her.

"And this?" Mia held up the small cup of tzatziki sauce.

"It's basically plain yogurt, dill, minced cucumber, and garlic."

Mia put the cup down.

"Taste it," Sydney said.

Mia could see that Sydney was trying to be patient with her, but that it was driving her crazy that she wouldn't even try anything. Mia sighed. She gingerly picked up her fork, put the very end of the fork into the sauce, and then brought it to her mouth. She was pleasantly surprised at the fresh taste to the sauce. She watched as Sydney picked up the round pita and all its contents like a taco and took a bite.

"So what's in yours?" Mia asked.

"Gyros," Sydney said when she'd swallowed. "It's pressed lamb"

"Oh."

"You want to try a piece?"

Mia shook her head.

"Do you like the tzatziki?" Sydney had noted that Mia hadn't made a face then.

"It's pretty good." Mia said, nodding.

"You could try it on the pita," Sydney suggested.

"Should I eat it like you do?"

"Or you can tear pieces off and pick up what you want." Sydney demonstrated by tearing a piece off the round pita on Mia's plate and picking up some chicken. "Do you like cucumber?"

Mia nodded. "And lettuce. Not tomato though."

"Okay." Sydney picked up a piece of lettuce and a piece of cucumber with her fork and added it to the pinch of pita bread and chicken, then dipped the end in the tzatziki and held it up to Mia's lips.

Mia opened her mouth and Sydney fed her the piece. Mia chewed it up, and she had to admit it was pretty good.

"You like it?" Sydney asked.

"Yeah," Mia said, sounding surprised.

Sydney grinned. "We have a breakthrough, folks."

"Bite me," Mia sassed, even as she did what Sydney had done, tearing a piece of pita and picking up chicken, lettuce and cucumber and dipping it.

"Name the time and place, babe," Sydney said, winking at her.

They ate companionably for a couple of minutes.

"So your family is in Oregon?" Sydney asked.

"Yeah," Mia said, "and begging me to come home every other day."

"They miss you."

"They think my immortal soul is in danger," Mia said, rolling her eyes.

"Uh-oh," Sydney said. "Conservative?"

"And then some. Why do you think I ran off to be with the first boy that asked?"

"And they know that didn't work out?" Sydney asked gently.

"They know I'm not with him anymore."

Sydney nodded, looking speculative.

"And before you ask, no, I haven't told them about you. They'd probably flip their lids."

Sydney nodded again, her face inscrutable.

"What about your parents?" Mia asked. "Do they live here? You're from here, aren't you?" she asked then, realizing she didn't know.

"Yeah, I grew up in Pomona."

"That's near here?" Mia asked, still not knowing a lot about the area.

"Yeah, it's about thirty minutes east of here."

"And they know about you being gay?"

Sydney laughed out loud at that question. "Oh yeah, they know."

Mia narrowed her eyes. "Okay, there's a story there, isn't there?"

Sydney picked up her beer and drained the bottle. She held it up to the waitress, who nodded, smiling.

"So?" Mia asked.

"My parents are… well, let's say about as opposite from conservative as you can possibly get."

"Okay, explain that," Mia said as the waitress brought Sydney's second beer.

Sydney waited for the waitress to leave.

"The easiest way to explain it is that my parents are basically swingers."

"I-I'm sorry?" Mia stammered.

Sydney grinned widely. "Yeah, they do all kinds of crazy shit."

Mia blinked. "Like sexual stuff?" she asked, looking stunned.

Sydney's lips curled as she nodded. "Yeah. It was great fun in high school, never knowing if I could bring friends home 'cause God knew what they'd be doing."

"Like what?" Mia asked, sure Sydney must be exaggerating.

"Well, one day I came home from school, very fortunately alone, and they were having a 'party,' which entailed a lot of very naked people."

"Oh my God!" Mia exclaimed.

"Tell me about it. I was used to it though. I put my headphones in and went to my room, where I was generally safe."

"Why do I think the word 'generally' is meaningful here?"

Sydney chuckled. "That's where my coming-out story happened."

"Coming-out story?"

"Where I figured out I was gay," Sydney explained.

"How old were you?"

"Fifteen."

"And…" Mia prompted with a wary look.

"She was one of my parents' 'friends,'" Sydney said, using air quotes to indicate that she meant sex companions.

"Oh my God, how old was she?" Mia asked, thinking that the woman was middle aged or something awful.

"Well, keep in mind that my mom had me when she was like fifteen, when my dad and her ran away from home together." Sydney grinned at the look on Mia's face. "Anyway, this woman wasn't even that old; she was more like twenty."

"Oh." Mia looked a little relieved.

"Anyway, I had come home to find another party going on—fortunately everyone was clothed this time, but there was cocaine and pot circulating heavily."

"Your parents did drugs?" Mia asked, aghast.

Sydney laughed at Mia's expression. "Yeah."

"Sorry, go on," Mia said, realizing she was interrupting constantly.

"I went into the kitchen to grab something to eat in my room and a soda, and ran into this woman. She was really something…" Sydney's voice trailed off. "She was wearing this barely-there midriff top and a micro-mini jean skirt and thigh-high boots. Man…" She shook her head. "Of course, I made a complete idiot of myself and fumbled around for something to say, not even sure what I did say, but I also got the hell out of there fast." She lifted the beer to her lips, taking a long drink. "Later that night, I was asleep and she came into my room. She kissed me, and I swear I was in love!"

"That easy, huh?" Mia asked, grinning.

"Well, I was definitely into women, that was for damned sure." Sydney smiled broadly.

"So did you see her again after that?" Mia wondered if Sydney's parents were even aware of their party guest violating their daughter, not that Sydney seemed any the worse for it.

"Oh yeah," Sydney said. "She taught me a lot."

"Wow," Mia said, shaking her head. "I guess you and I really had different upbringings, huh?"

"I'd say so."

Later in the car, Sydney got a phone call. She answered it with the hands-free in the Z.

"Hello?"

"Syd?" replied a woman.

Sydney grinned. "Hi, Mom. What's up?" she asked, glancing over at Mia.

"We have a problem with the computer," Sydney's mother said.

Sydney rolled her eyes. "What's it doing this time?"

"Well, it won't come on, and the screen is all blue…"

Sydney chuckled. "That's called the blue screen of death, Mom. Jesus, that's three laptops in like three months!"

"I don't know what keeps happening!" Sydney's mother exclaimed anxiously.

"I do," Sydney said under her breath.

"What?"

"Nothing, Mom," Sydney said. "I can come by tomorrow after work and take a look at it."

"You can't come today?" her mom asked, sounding crestfallen.

Sydney blew her breath out, looking over at Mia. Mia nodded.

"Fine, Mom, I'll come today," she said. "But my bet is we'll be buying you two yet another laptop."

Sydney's mother sighed. "Oh, hold on, Sydney. Your dad wants to talk to you."

"Oh, good," Sydney said, sounding far from happy about the prospect.

"Syd!" boomed a man's voice.

"Hi, Dad," Sydney said, grinning.

"Syd, I want to get an Alienware like yours," he said enthusiastically.

Sydney actually glowered at the display on her phone, making Mia laugh.

"No, just… no," Sydney said.

"What? Why?" her dad said, his voice actually whiney.

Sydney looked at her phone, all authority.

"Because I'm not going to pronounce time of death on an Alienware when you kill it in the month you usually kill them in, Dad. That would be complete sacrilege."

"But…" he began in a beseeching tone. "I want to get into gaming with some of the guys and—"

"No," Sydney said again. "You are not going to kill an Alienware, Dad. It's just not going to happen, so give it up."

"I can buy one if I want," her father said petulantly.

"You can," Sydney said, her eyes glittering with mischief. "And who's going to set it up for you?"

"Well…" he stammered. "I can get one of my friends to do it," he said triumphantly.

"Go for it," Sydney said immediately, her lips curling into a sardonic grin.

There was silence on the other end of the phone.

"You're saying that you won't mind?" her father asked.

"I'm saying go ahead and spend 3K on a computer and get one of your little friends to set it up for ya, Dad."

Again there was silence.

"I don't like you right now," came the next comment. "Here's your mother."

Sydney started laughing, shaking her head. "Mom, tell Dad to just calm down. I'll be over in an hour, okay?"

"Okay," Sydney's mother said, also sounding somewhat amused. "See you soon, honey."

Sydney disconnected the call.

"Are they always like that?" Mia asked.

Sydney pushed her lower lip out, considering, then nodded. "Pretty much."

"So it's like you're the parent and they're the teenagers?"

"Yeah, pretty much," Sydney repeated.

"Wow," Mia said. "So how can they afford three thousand-dollar computers? Or any computers, for that matter."

"My dad runs a very successful bar, and my mother is actually a pretty successful costume designer for TV shows."

"Oh," Mia said, looking surprised again.

"Yeah, they just like to stay young. And they got used to me being totally responsible, so they rely on me a lot."

Mia nodded, thinking that must have been hard on her as a kid. "Kind of a rough childhood?"

Sydney shrugged. "Nah. I didn't have to deal with a lot of parental interference, and they were always supportive of me. I'll take that over parents I have to run away from any day," she said, winking at Mia.

"I see your point," Mia said, grinning.

Three hours later, Mia left Sydney's childhood home, absolutely adoring Sydney's parents and knowing that Sydney had so much more going on in her life than she'd realized. Ellen and RayRay Carson were very definite characters, but it was obvious they loved their daughter dearly, and she loved them too.

There had been a comical conversation between Sydney and her father about the computer, where Sydney explained to him the differences between the different types of computers. In the meantime, Ellen had told Mia over and over again what a beautiful girl she was. It got to the point where Sydney had walked over, taking Mia's hand and pulling her close to her, and given her mother a narrowed look.

"She's with me, Mom, so back off. I don't wanna have to kill ya."

"Maybe she prefers older women," Ellen had replied, winking at Mia.

"She prefers me," Sydney told her mother.

"Is that true, Mia?" Ellen asked.

"I really do have a thing for Syd," Mia said, smiling.

Ellen sighed sadly, shaking her head.

Sydney laughed, shaking her head too. "Always on the make," she muttered.

Chapter 6

Sable crawled into bed behind Jocelyn, having heard her coughing.

"Jocelyn, are you okay?" Sable asked, reaching out to touch Jocelyn's shoulder.

Jocelyn turned over. "I don't feel too good."

Grimacing, Sable touched Jocelyn's forehead. "You feel warm," she said, getting out of bed.

She got the thermometer and put it in Jocelyn's ear, touching the button. When it beeped, she looked at it. She grimaced again.

"A hundred and one, babe. We should probably take you to the hospital."

"Let's try some Tylenol first, okay?" Jocelyn said.

Sable looked back at her, not wanting to agree, but knowing that Jocelyn was just tired of feeling lousy, and going to the hospital meant tests and sitting around.

"Okay," Sable said.

Two hours later, Sable saw that Jocelyn's breathing was labored, even though she was asleep.

Touching Jocelyn's shoulder, she shook her gently. "Babe?"

"Hmm?" Jocelyn murmured tiredly.

"Your breathing is labored. I'm worried."

Jocelyn turned over onto her back, taking a few deep breaths and coughing some. Finally she nodded.

"Something's not right. Let's go," Jocelyn said, sounding resigned.

Sable got her up and called for Jake, who helped her get Jocelyn into the SUV.

Gage and Kit were asleep when Gage's phone rang. Reaching over, she picked it up. Kit sat up. She could only hear Gage's side of the conversation.

"Hello? Yeah, this is Gage McGinnis… Yes… She's where? Okay what happened?" she asked, with a worried glance at Kit. "Okay, well, I'll be right down. Thank you."

After Gage hung up, Kit asked, "What was that about?"

"That was Cedars. Gun was brought into Emergency." She got out of bed and started to pull on her jeans.

"What! What happened?" Kit asked.

"Don't know. They said that they called me because I'm on her emergency contacts, but Sable brought her in."

"Do you want me to come with you?" Kit asked, already trying to figure out what she'd do about Caitlyn.

"No," Gage said. "It's okay, babe. Caitlyn is here; if she wakes up you need to be here. God only knows what kind of stupor my mom is in at this point."

"Okay," Kit said. "She'll be okay, Gage," she said, referring to Jocelyn.

Gage drew in a deep breath as she sat down to pull on her combat boots. "I hope so."

An hour after they'd gotten to the ER, Jocelyn was in a room, and things moved fast for Sable Sands. The doctor had told Sable that Jocelyn had pneumonia. It was common during chemotherapy—the body's immune system was compromised, so it was easy to get infections.

"We're giving her a breathing treatment and some medications that should help clear her lungs. You can see her in about a half hour," the doctor told her.

"Okay, thank you," Sable said.

She'd gone down to the cafeteria to get coffee and was on her way back to the waiting room when she saw Gage. She glanced over at Jake, who had, as usual, trailed her everywhere she went. His lips twitched when he saw Gage. It was hard to miss the stride and fiery red hair. Sable stopped dead in her tracks, just as Gage looked up and saw her. Gage strode over to her.

"What the hell happened?" Gage demanded immediately.

"Gage, what are you doing here?" Sable asked, stalling for time.

Gage smiled maliciously. "I'm still Gun's emergency contact," she said, her voice icy. "Now answer my fucking question. What is going on?"

Sable stared at Gage, surprised by Gage's open hostility. She noticed that Jake took a step toward her; she shook her head at him. There was no way she was going to allow was for Jake to hurt Gage when Gage had every right to be pissed at her.

She opened the lid to her coffee, blowing on it to cool it, while her mind raced. She had no idea what to tell Gage at this point.

"Tell me what's going on with Gun," Gage gritted out, annoyed by Sable's casual attitude.

"She's fine, Gage," Sable said. "She wasn't feeling well tonight and had a fever. Later she couldn't breathe really well, so we went ahead and came down. They said she has pneumonia. They're giving her a breathing treatment and some meds. No big deal." Her tone indicated that Gage was overreacting.

Gage heard the tone and narrowed her eyes at Sable. She could sense the undercurrent, and the cop in her said something else was going on.

"There's more to it than that," Gage said.

"There really isn't," Sable said airily.

"I don't believe you." With that, Gage turned to walk toward the bed that Jocelyn was in.

"Where are you going?" Sable exclaimed as she moved to stop Gage.

"I'm going to go check on my partner, and you're going to get the hell out of my way," Gage said sharply.

"They said we can't see her yet," Sable said, sounding desperate now.

Gage's green eyes were points of fire as she narrowed them again. "Sable, get out of my way before I remove you from my path," she said, her tone a low threat. "I'm not the gentleman Gun is—I'll knock you out to get you out of my way. So move," she said, the last as a growl.

Sable jumped out of her way. She put out her hand to Jake to halt him from stopping Gage. She didn't want Gage hurt; it was bad enough that they'd been hiding it from her all of this time. Gage strode down the hallway and turned. Sable rushed after her, thinking Jocelyn was going to kill her. When Sable caught up to Gage she was standing staring down at Jocelyn. As Sable watched mutely, Gage touched the bruises on the inside of Jocelyn's elbow, her lips curling in distaste.

"Are you two fucking shooting now?" Gage asked, her eyes ablaze as she glared at Sable.

"What?" Sable replied. "Jesus, no. I don't do that shit."

"So she's doing it alone?" Gage asked doubtfully.

"She's not doing anything. Those are from the IV," Sable said, realizing too late that Jocelyn didn't have an IV in at that point.

"What IV?" Gage asked.

"I—" Sable stammered, but she was interrupted by the doctor coming into the room.

"She's responding well to the treatment," the doctor said, not sensing the tension in the room at all, "and the good news is it shouldn't interfere with her next round of—"

"Doctor!" Sable exclaimed, cutting him off.

"Next round of what?" Gage snapped, seeing that Sable was trying to usher the doctor out.

"The next round—Erg! Why are you pushing me?" he asked as Sable physically pushed him out of the room.

"What the fuck is he talking about?" Gage yelled at Sable the moment she returned to the room. "Next round of what?"

"Chemo," Jocelyn said from the bed, her voice weak.

Gage's head snapped around so fast she felt her vision swim. "What?" she asked breathlessly as she staggered.

"Gage!" Sable exclaimed; Gage actually looked like she was going to pass out.

Jake moved to Gage, ushering her to the chair next to the bed. Gage sat with her legs wide apart as she did her best to recover from the shock she'd just received. Jocelyn was watching her, concern on her face. It hit Gage harder then, seeing Jocelyn worried about her, when she was obviously sick...

"For what?" Gage finally managed to ask, her voice barely audible.

Jocelyn grimaced slightly, and Gage knew the answer before she said it.

"Ovarian cancer," Jocelyn said. Gage closed her eyes.

"Jesus…" Gage breathed, feeling her chest constrict, then she opened her eyes. "What stage?"

"Between one and two," she said gently.

"Surgery?"

"Had it."

Gage's eyes widened. "Your 'vacation'?"

Jocelyn's lips twitched as she nodded.

Gage shook her head. "Jesus, Jos, why didn't you tell me?"

Jocelyn looked back at her. "Because I knew if I told you, you'd implode your life to save me."

Gage blinked a few times, then she winced as she nodded. She knew that Jocelyn was right, that she'd done exactly that previously, and it had never been life and death like this. Then she looked over at Sable.

"I guess that's why you two moved in together?"

Sable nodded.

"And why you were heard throwing up in the bathroom at work?" Gage said to Jocelyn. "And this?" She gestured to Jocelyn's arm.

"I did my first round of chemo a week and a half ago. The side effects have been hanging on."

"And now this," Gage said, gesturing to where they were.

Jocelyn nodded.

"God, Jos," Gage said, looking between Jocelyn and Sable. "You two were dealing with all of this all by yourselves?"

"Gage," Sable said, seeing that Jocelyn was getting tired, "let's go outside and talk, okay? Jocelyn needs to get some rest."

Gage glanced sharply at Jocelyn when she heard Sable use her full name. Jocelyn only grinned.

"Don't start," Jocelyn said simply, her voice indeed showing fatigue.

Gage stood up, stepping over to the side of the bed. She put her hand to Jocelyn's head, her thumb brushing over her forehead, her eyes staring into Jocelyn's.

"You and me, we're going to talk when you get out of here," she said, then she kissed Jocelyn's forehead. "I love you."

Jocelyn smiled tiredly. "Love you."

Gage looked at Sable as she stood up, gesturing with her head toward the door. They walked out together, with Jake trailing behind. Gage led Sable out to the smoking area and immediately lit a cigarette with shaking hands. Jake and Sable exchanged glances.

"How did the surgery go?" Gage asked when she'd had a chance to collect herself.

"They think they got it all," Sable said.

Gage nodded, her mind racing, going back over things in her head. Then she looked at Sable.

"She knew... Before you came back, she knew..."

Sable nodded.

"That's why she was off the rails like that," Gage said, shaking her head. "I mean, I know the original spin was because of you, but she stepped it up at one point, and that's when I called you. That must have been when she found out... she said her stomach had been bothering her... Fuck! I should have seen that!"

"How could you have?"

Gage grimaced. "I guess she didn't tell you, huh?"

"Tell me what?"

"Her mother died of ovarian cancer. We did a lot of research during that time, know way more about it than either of us ever wanted to know, including the symptoms and warning signs. My guess is either Jos was ignoring them or just didn't equate it somehow."

Sable closed her eyes slowly, her lips trembling. "She said she didn't see the point in putting the people she loved through a fight, just so she could die anyway…"

Gage swallowed at hearing how desolate Jocelyn had been and how easy it would have been for her to have given in and given up.

"So she wasn't going to get treatment?"

"No," Sable said.

Gage looked at Sable for a long moment. "And I guess I have you to thank for her changing her mind?"

"I don't know that it was me," Sable said. "I just told her I'd help her as much as she needed."

"And she's been letting you take care of her?" Gage asked, amazed.

Sable nodded, seeing the surprise on Gage's face.

"And you're also getting away with calling her Jocelyn…"

"I think she gave up trying to stop me," Sable said, grinning.

"Yeah…" Gage said, dragging the word out. "Gun doesn't give up too often."

Sable shrugged. "She's in a more important battle this time."

Gage nodded slowly. "Well, we need to talk about how we want to handle things moving forward."

"Things are working fine," Sable said far too quickly, her tone defensive.

Gage held up her hand. "I'm not saying they aren't, Sable. I'm saying that I don't want her killing herself to get in to work if she's not up to it. I also want to help with whatever I can, okay?" she said earnestly. "You've been doing this amazing thing, all by yourself, Sable." She reached out to touch Sable's cheek. "And it looks like you haven't really been taking care of yourself. So let me and Kit and our friends help you, okay?"

143

Sable knew that her fear of Gage taking over, and her fear that Jocelyn really wanted that, was at the front of her mind. She nodded slowly, doing her best not to feel the loss of having Jocelyn all to herself. She knew that Gage was important to Jocelyn; she was just worried that Gage was *too* important to Jocelyn.

Gage could see the emotions warring in Sable's eyes. She knew that Sable Sands was in love with Jocelyn. She wasn't surprised; Jocelyn was a force unto herself when she drew people in to her. Gage could only imagine that seeing Jocelyn so vulnerable was like a giant magnet pulling Sable in—seeing someone as strong as Jocelyn being helpless was highly attractive. It wasn't something many people had ever seen with Jocelyn. In fact, no one else had seen it but Gage.

Gage was still thinking about that as she drove back to her mother's house. It started hitting her when she got off the freeway that her best friend in the entire world had cancer. The same kind of cancer that had killed her mother, and they'd caught her cancer early too. By the time Gage pulled into her mother's garage, she felt sick.

Walking into the house, she went straight to the liquor cabinet and poured herself a couple of shots, downing them in succession. She replaced the decanter with shaking hands and walked down the hall to the bedroom she was sharing with Kit. She took her jeans off in the dark, sitting down to unlace her boots and kick them off.

"Gage?" Kit queried from the bed.

"Yeah." Gage got up and climbed into bed.

"Is everything okay?" Kit smelled alcohol on Gage's breath immediately, and her stomach lurched.

Gage took Kit into her arms, placing her head against the front of Kit's shoulder.

"Jos has cancer," she said simply.

"Oh God!" Kit said, tears in her eyes instantly.

Then Gage was crying and holding on to her like she was a life raft in stormy seas. Kit held her, stroking her hair and doing her best to soothe her. When Gage calmed down, they talked about what Gage knew.

"It sounds like she's doing well," Kit said. "And it sounds like Sable is way more awesome than we thought," she said with a smile.

Gage chuckled softly. "Yeah…"

"So why didn't she tell you?"

"'Cause she knows me."

"What does that mean?" Kit asked.

"It means that it's been her experience that when she needs me, I drop everything to be there for her," Gage said. "And that's been stuff like a bad day at work or a shitty boss. It's never been life and death before."

Kit nodded, taking a deep breath.

"And she's right." Gage shook her head ruefully. "I drop everything, no matter what."

Again Kit nodded, her look resigned as she started to sit up.

Gage caught not only the look but Kit's move to distance herself from Gage.

Gage stopped Kit's movement. "Babe, wait."

"It's okay," Kit said, doing her best to hold back tears. "I understand."

"No, you don't," Gage said, sitting up and touching Kit's face. "I'm saying that's why Jocelyn didn't tell me. I'm not saying that's what's going to happen, okay?"

"But this is life and death."

"And she has Sable. And I have you, and I need you especially right now. Okay?"

Kit smiled. "Then there's nowhere else I'd want to be."

145

"Good," Gage said, leaning in to kiss her, and continuing to kiss her as things got heated.

"Ugh!" Gage exclaimed as she remembered that Caitlyn was in the house. She lay back, pulling Kit down with her.

"You know what we need to do," Gage said, stroking Kit's hair. "We need to buy a house."

Kit turned to her. "A house?"

"Yeah," Gage said. "Something for you, me and Caitlyn." She smiled.

"We can do that," Kit said. "Now that I make some more money and don't have to pay off Jack's bills, I can afford to help with a house payment."

Gage nodded slowly. "And you know what else I think we should do?"

"What?"

"I think we should get married."

"What?" Kit asked again.

Gage smiled at the look of surprise on Kit's face. She reached up to touch Kit's cheek, her eyes staring into Kit's.

"Will you marry me, Kit?"

"Really?" Kit asked, her blue eyes wide.

Gage laughed softly. "Yes, really."

"Oh, Gage," Kit said, touching Gage's hand on her cheek. "I would love to be your wife."

"Would you let me adopt Caitlyn?" Gage asked.

Kit looked shocked. "You'd want to adopt Caitlyn?"

"As long as it would be okay with you. If it wouldn't be, I understa—"

Kit interrupted her by pressing her lips to Gage's. "Yes," she said against Gage's mouth. "Yes, yes, yes…"

Jocelyn watched with an amused look on her face as Sable moved around the master bedroom.

"Will you just ditch somewhere?" she asked, grinning.

"Ditch?" Sable asked.

"Land," Jocelyn explained.

Sable bit her lip. "I just want to make sure everything's okay and you're okay."

Jocelyn smiled. "Then come here and see if I'm okay."

Sable walked over to the bed and sat down. Jocelyn took her arm and pulled Sable down on the bed with her, leaning in to kiss her. She touched Sable's cheek, then slid her hand to the back of Sable's head, deepening the kiss. Sable moaned against her lips; they hadn't been together sexually in weeks, and her body had just come alive at the exquisite pressure of Jocelyn's lips on hers.

In minutes they were making love, and Sable was once again reminded of how incredible their sexual chemistry was, over and over again. Afterwards, they lay catching their breath, Jocelyn still lying partially over Sable.

"Oh yeah, I remember this..." Jocelyn grinned as she propped herself up on one elbow.

Sable chuckled gently, her fingers flexing on Jocelyn's back. In one move, Jocelyn rolled to her back, taking Sable with her so that Sable ended up over her.

They lay together for a while, not talking, just lying there, each lost in her own thoughts.

"Mmm, we need to get ahold of Gage," Jocelyn said offhandedly.

"Why?"

"She said that we needed to talk when I got out of the hospital. So I figured we should call her now that I'm home," Jocelyn said with a shrug.

Sable nodded. "Okay, I'll give her a call."

"Cool."

Jocelyn fell asleep shortly thereafter, and Sable carefully got up and pulled her bathrobe on, going into the other room to make some calls.

Jocelyn woke the next morning and was staring up at the ceiling when Sable entered the room. She was talking on her cell phone as she looked over at Jocelyn. Sable walked across the room to look out the window, nodding to the person on the phone.

"Yeah, okay…" she was saying. "That should work… okay. Let me know what they say. Yeah, call me back. Thanks." With that she hung up.

"What was that?" Jocelyn asked as she sat up.

Sable glanced at her cautiously. "It was my agent."

Jocelyn held her arm out to indicate she wanted Sable to come sit with her. Sable did so.

"So what did he want?" Jocelyn leaned back against the head-board, her arm encircling Sable's shoulders and pulling her into her side.

Sable rested her head against the hollow of Jocelyn's shoulder, taking a slow, deep breath before answering.

"He wants me to do some show dates to promote my new album," she said, her voice purposely even.

"When does he expect you to do that?" Jocelyn asked warily.

Sable shrugged. "The album comes out in two months, so probably soon."

"And where does he want you to do them?"

"Well, the album is dropping in London first, so…"

"So you're going back to London," Jocelyn said.

Sable looked up at her, surprised by the caustic tone in Jocelyn's voice.

"Well, I would need to…" Sable trailed off as Jocelyn sat up, her arm dropping from Sable's shoulders.

"So you're leaving again?" Jocelyn clarified.

"I need to—"

"You're leaving again," Jocelyn said, more sharply this time.

"Jocelyn…" Sable began placatingly.

"Don't fucking try it, Sable," Jocelyn snapped.

"Try what?" Sable asked, surprised by Jocelyn's sudden anger.

"Don't try lying to me about why you're running again," Jocelyn said, her expression livid. "You're running because I said we needed to call Gage, and you think that means that I want her here instead of you. So you're going to run before I can tell you I want you to leave."

Sable's chocolate-brown eyes searched Jocelyn's. Her mind was racing; Jocelyn could see it.

Sable shook her head. "I don't know what—"

"I said don't fucking lie to me, Sable, and I meant it!" Jocelyn snapped, her eyes blazing in fury as her hand clapped over Sable's mouth. "You still fucking think that I want Gage. You still think that I'm in love with her, don't you?"

Sable's eyes reflected fear at Jocelyn's anger. Even so, she nodded slowly.

"Jesus!" Jocelyn exclaimed, snatching her hand away from Sable's mouth like she'd been burned. "You've gotta be fucking kidding me!" Shaking her head in disbelief, she turned to Sable, her face a mask of anger and incredulity. "After all of this…" She shook her head again. "You don't get it. You just don't…"

149

"What don't I get?" Sable asked, her voice tremulous, her lips trembling. She was sure this was the part where Jocelyn was going to tell her how she could never mean to her what Gage did and that she just needed to get used to that.

Jocelyn turned to look at her, putting her face next to Sable's.

"That I'm not in love with Gage, because I'm in love with you." Jocelyn's voice was so soft that Sable wondered if she'd misunderstood. Jocelyn pulled back, looking into Sable's eyes. "Because I love you, Sable... you and only you."

Sable's eyes widened significantly and then closed slowly as she took in what Jocelyn had said. Suddenly she threw her arms around Jocelyn's neck and burst into tears. Jocelyn was shocked by the action but put her arms around Sable, holding her as she cried.

When Sable quieted, Jocelyn looked down at her. "Jesus, I didn't think it was such bad news," she said sardonically.

Sable lifted her head and fastened her lips to Jocelyn's in a deep and passionate kiss. Jocelyn held her close, kissing her back. Slowly but surely, Sable pushed Jocelyn back on the bed, moving over her, pressing close and sliding her hands down Jocelyn's body.

Jocelyn shuddered at the feel of Sable's hands on her. Sable continued to touch her until Jocelyn was trembling with need.

"Baby, please..." Jocelyn begged.

Sable put her lips near Jocelyn's ear. "Tell me again," she whispered.

"I love you," Jocelyn groaned in reply.

Only then did Sable bring her to release. Jocelyn came with a shout that caused a shudder in Sable. Jocelyn quickly returned the favor.

"By the way," Sable said, her voice still breathless, as she glanced at the clock on the wall. "Gage will be here at noon."

Jocelyn glanced at the clock too; it was ten. She turned onto her side, pulling Sable into her arms and curling her body around hers.

"Can I tell you how much I love it when you do that?" Sable said softly, putting her arms over Jocelyn's that were wrapped around her.

"Good, 'cause I love doing it," Jocelyn said, nuzzling Sable's neck.

"I love you," Sable said.

"I know."

Sable turned over, looking up at her. "You do?" she asked, shocked.

"Why else would you go through all of this with me?" Jocelyn asked, shaking her head in wonder.

Sable smiled, then kissed Jocelyn's neck. They lay together for a while, not talking.

"Jocelyn?" Sable queried softly.

"Do you know how many people are allowed to call me that?"

"How many?"

"Exactly one."

"Me?" Sable asked, grinning.

"Yep. What?"

"When did you know you loved me?"

"After you left the first time," Jocelyn said.

"Really?" Sable looked over her shoulder at Jocelyn.

"Why do you think I went off the deep end?" Jocelyn asked. "I didn't find out about the cancer till about long after you left."

Sable shook her head in wonder. "Why didn't you tell me before that you loved me?"

Jocelyn's gaze flickered. "I wanted to wait…" She trailed off as Sable's head snapped up.

"Wait until what?" Sable asked, her tone sharp because she was sure she already knew.

Jocelyn looked down at her, her eyes saying *You know*. Sable grimaced, tears in her eyes instantly.

"You wanted to wait to see if you'd die or not," Sable said, tears in her voice as well.

Jocelyn's eyes were both apologetic and sad as she nodded.

"Jocelyn," Sable said, reaching up to touch Jocelyn's face, "you aren't going to die. I won't let you."

Jocelyn shook her head. "You don't understand."

"I do understand," Sable said. "Gage told me about your mother. I'm so sorry that you lost her, but I won't lose you."

Jocelyn's look told her that she may not have a choice.

"I won't lose you," Sable said again, in a stronger tone.

"I really don't want to die," Jocelyn said tremulously.

"I just found you. I'm not going to lose you."

Sable hugged Jocelyn to her. Jocelyn slid her arms tighter around Sable, holding her tight.

Later that afternoon, Gage and Kit arrived at the house. Sable and Jocelyn were sitting out on the patio. Jocelyn was smoking.

"Oh, that looks healthy," Gage said, making a face at Jocelyn.

"Bite me."

Gage noted that Jocelyn's hand was in Sable's; she grinned.

"So, we have something to tell you," Gage said, taking Kit's hand in hers.

"What's that?" Jocelyn asked.

"We're getting married." Gage's green eyes were shining.

"Hooah!" Jocelyn smiled as she stood up and hugged Gage, kissing her cheek, and then reached over to hug Kit. "Congratulations."

"Congratulations!" Sable said, smiling brightly. She could see that Jocelyn was happy for Gage. It was obvious. Any doubts she would have still had were resoundingly extinguished.

"Now," Gage said, sitting down in the chair across from Jocelyn, "let's talk about how we're going to get you healthy so you can be my best woman at my wedding."

They spent the next three hours talking about who they would tell at the office, and how they'd handle Jocelyn's illness and insure she'd get enough rest without making herself crazy with boredom.

***

Two days later at the office, Jocelyn and Gage met with Harley, Shiloh, Shenin, Sebastian, Kashena and Jack.

"What's goin' on?" Sebastian asked Kashena on their way to Gage's office.

"Got me," Kashena said, shrugging.

"What's this about?" Harley asked the other two as they met up outside Gage's office.

Kashena and Sebastian both shook their heads.

"You know?" Kashena asked Shenin as she walked up.

"Nope," Shenin said. "Let's go find out."

In Gage's office sat Kit, Jocelyn, Sable and Gage, all looking fairly serious. The other six sat down. There was a long silence.

"Okay, what the hell is going on?" Sebastian asked, not liking the tension in the room.

Kashena and Shenin looked at each other, then back at Gage.

Gage blew her breath out, nodding at Jocelyn.

Jocelyn looked at the group. "I have cancer," she said simply.

"What!" Shenin exclaimed, standing up to hug Jocelyn immediately.

Jocelyn smiled as she hugged Shenin.

"What kind of cancer?" Sebastian asked warily.

"Ovarian," Sable told him.

"Treatment?" Kashena asked.

"Yeah," Jocelyn said as Shenin sat back down. "I already had surgery, and my first round of chemo."

"That's why you were throwing up…" Harley said.

"Yeah," Jocelyn said.

"Why didn't you tell us sooner?" Shiloh asked, looking worried.

"Because she knew I'd freak out," Gage said, glancing at Jocelyn, "and she was trying to protect me."

Shiloh nodded, understanding that answer. She glanced at Harley. She could see that Harley was processing what was happening. It hadn't really hit her yet.

"So how can we help?" Jack asked.

"Well," Gage began, looking at Jack, "you're going to be key in keeping an eye on her for us." She gave Jocelyn a sidelong look. "Gun's not one to take care of herself…"

"And that's going to change as of now," Sable said, giving Jocelyn a stern look.

Jocelyn quirked her lips in a partial grimace.

"Does the rest of the group know?" Sebastian asked.

"No," Gage said, but then held up her hand. "Not out of design. Just because we're telling you guys first."

Kashena, Sebastian and Shenin all nodded.

"I can take point on some of the projects Jos is working on," Harley said. "I can definitely take that FisCal garbage off her desk."

Jocelyn smiled. "And I will love you forever."

154

The group talked for a while longer about what could be taken off Jocelyn's shoulders for the duration of her treatment. Gage's ideal was that Jocelyn be kept in the loop, but that she wouldn't be saddled with everything. Once again, Gage was astounded by the women and man she'd brought into her agency. These people understood the concept of loyalty and commitment to a cause.

As the meeting wrapped up, Jocelyn looked at Gage pointedly. "Don't you have something else to tell them?"

Gage grinned, glancing at Kit. She held her hand out to Kit, who took it, biting her lip as she looked at the people in the room.

"Kit and I are getting married," Gage said, smiling.

"Hooah!" Sebastian said as he got up to congratulate them.

"Oh my God, that's fantastic!" Shenin said.

Everyone was happy for the two, hugging and congratulating them.

"Now, let's get through this other thing," Kashena said, winking at Jocelyn, "so we can have a party."

"I hear that," Jocelyn said with a grin.

Two days later, Jocelyn was starting to get used to the level of harassment she was going to receive while people took care of her.

"Sable called," Jack said as he handed her papers to sign. "She said to make sure you take your pill."

Jocelyn looked at the clock. "I can't until two."

"Okay," he said, glancing at the clock too; it was 1 p.m. "Oh, and Gage sent this." He handed her some pork jerky, which was black-cherry barbecue flavor.

Jocelyn smiled. "Oh… she does love me."

"Just take it slow," Jack said, passing her the bottle of water he'd gotten her from the kitchen.

"Yes, dear," Jocelyn said as she winked at him.

Two hours later, Jack walked in and saw that Jocelyn was looking nauseous.

"Not agreeing with you?" Jack asked, moving to Jocelyn's side, taking her right arm in his hand and using the pressure point Sable had shown him to combat Jocelyn's nausea.

Jocelyn shook her head, even as she smiled slightly at Jack's hold on her arm.

"Did you take your pill?" Jack asked.

"Shit," Jocelyn muttered.

"Where is it?"

Jocelyn took it out of her jacket pocket, holding it up and popping it out of the blister pack.

"Got it, Mom." She dropped the pill under her tongue to let it dissolve.

"Hey did you—Are you feeling sick?" Gage asked, seeing Jack holding Jocelyn's arm.

"Yeah," Jocelyn said. "Just took my pill."

"Aren't you supposed to stay ahead of that?" Gage grinned as she walked into Jocelyn's office and sat down in the chair across from Jocelyn's desk.

"Bite me," Jocelyn said, grinning back.

"None of that, girls," Jack inserted, his smile wry.

"Jealous?" Jocelyn asked.

Jack winked. "Not unless Sebastian is involved."

Jocelyn laughed at that one. "I wouldn't say that too loud."

"Baz might find it amusing," Gage said, laughing. "Did you get the jerky?"

"I did, thank you," Jocelyn said. "Where did you find that?"

"Kit found it. She heard you had a thing for cherry."

"I do love that girl," Jocelyn said. "You better marry her fast."

"Back off, you got your own," Gage said, winking at Jocelyn.

"Yes, yes I do," Jocelyn said, smiling fondly.

"Did you tell her yet?" Gage asked as she put her feet up on Jocelyn's desk. It felt good to be talking like old times again.

"Tell her what?" Jocelyn asked, her face inscrutable.

"That you're in love with her," Gage said with a smirk.

Jocelyn stared at her, surprise reflected in her eyes.

"You never let anyone call you Jocelyn, not even me," Gage said. "The one time I called you that you almost busted me in the mouth. She calls you it and you don't bat an eyelash. That's love, my friend."

"You're in love with Sable Sands…" Jack said. "That's pretty tight."

Jocelyn grinned, looking somewhat embarrassed.

"I'm happy for ya, Gun," Gage said. "It's about damned time."

"Look who's talking," Jocelyn said.

"Gives you a helluva reason to kick cancer's ass, doesn't it?" Gage said, her eyes narrowing a little.

Jocelyn grimaced. "I'm guessing she told you, huh?"

Jack noted the more serious looks going on and wisely absented himself from the office quietly.

"Yeah," Gage said.

Jocelyn nodded, looking apologetic.

"You'd leave Mark and me just like that?" Gage asked.

"When's the last time we've even seen Mark?"

"Doesn't matter, Jos. He's still our son."

It was true that Mark hadn't been around much since his baby had been born. It broke both Gage's and Jocelyn's hearts, but his girlfriend wasn't interested in sharing their baby with his lesbian mothers. They were hoping it would change, but at that point it hadn't.

"I just didn't want to go out like my mother did, Jock," Jocelyn said.

Jocelyn's mother had fought long and hard against cancer, and had basically faded away. From what they'd been told, she'd been in so much pain that she'd suffered terribly right up until the end. Because Jocelyn's parents were religious and abhorred the fact that their daughter was gay, Jocelyn hadn't been allowed to see her mother before she died. It had hurt her all the same.

"I know, Gun, but it's not going to be like that, okay? It's not," Gage said. "We're going to take care of you. All of us. Okay?"

Jocelyn took a deep breath and nodded.

Chapter 7

It was Saturday night, and Sydney was picking Mia up from the club. She'd wanted to wait outside, but the manager had seen her sitting in her car and told her to come in, that he'd buy her a drink. Sydney didn't want to be rude to the man, so she finally gave in and followed him inside.

She did her best not to look around—the last thing she wanted to see was Mia dancing for some guy. Sydney knew it was bad that it was bothering her more what Mia did for a living, and she knew it wasn't likely to get better. She'd basically tried to avoid seeing Mia right after she'd gotten off work, and very definitely avoided coming to the club. On this particular night, however, Mia's car wasn't running right, so she'd asked Sydney if she could pick her up. Sydney really hadn't had a choice; of course she had to do it.

As Sydney stood with her back to the stages, she could hear a ruckus.

"Damn it," the manager muttered. "I'll be right back."

Sydney gritted her teeth, hearing a guy getting verbally lewd, and then she heard the one thing she didn't want to hear—she heard Mia's voice yell "Stop!"

"Son of a…" Sydney turned around and strode over to where the commotion was occurring.

Exactly as Sydney had feared, a man had his hand clamped around Mia's wrist and was attempting to pull her off the stage. He'd already decked the manager, who was lying on the ground. Sydney lashed out with a booted foot and kicked the guy square in the nuts from behind. He instantly released Mia and howled in pain as he dropped to his knees. Sydney took Mia's hand, pulling her closer, then lifted her down from the stage and led her to the backroom.

Inside the room, Sydney turned to Mia, pulling her into her arms.

"Are you okay?" Sydney asked.

"I'm okay," Mia said.

"Hey! Next time how about letting me do my job?" the bouncer said angrily from behind them.

Sydney's head snapped around. "How about you get around to fucking doing your job before I have to and my girl gets accosted!"

The bouncer took a menacing step toward Sydney, and her chin came up instantly. Mia stepped between them.

"You were a little slow on the response time there, Bill," Mia said. "The guy even had time to deck Harry." She used her best and most charming smile on the man, and Sydney saw him get all hot and bothered. Her lips twitched in annoyance. The shit never stopped with men…

"I'm gonna go outside," Sydney said, disgust in her voice.

Mia found Sydney sitting on the hood of her car, smoking a cigarette, half an hour later.

"Everything okay?" Mia asked hesitantly, noting a number of butts on the ground.

Again, Sydney's lips twitched. Moving off the hood, she dropped her cigarette and stubbed it out. She walked over and opened the passenger door of the car. Mia reached up to kiss her, but Sydney pulled her head back.

"Not while you smell like men," Sydney said, trying to keep her voice even.

"Wow!" Mia said, looking shocked.

160

Sydney winced, knowing that her attitude about Mia's job was coming out because of the incident, and the fact that she'd just caught a whiff of some guy's sweat on her girlfriend and it was making her feel sick.

"I'm sorry," Sydney said, still holding the door open for Mia.

Mia got into the car, and sat feeling a little surprised by Sydney's attitude. The men she'd dated had gotten off on the fact that she was a dancer; she guessed this was yet another difference between dating men and dating women. Mia's irritation got the better of her as Sydney turned toward her apartment.

"I think I want to go back to my place," Mia said.

Sydney glanced at her in surprise, then she nodded, flipping a U-turn at the next light and accelerating sharply into the turn, her tires squealing.

Mia saw that the muscles in Sydney's jaw were twitching, which meant she was clenching her teeth.

"So you have a problem with my job now?" Mia asked accusingly.

Sydney didn't answer at first, then sniffed in irritation. "I have a problem with my girlfriend smelling like men when she gets off work, yeah."

"You forget how you met me?"

"Nope," Sydney said. "Just like to forget that you do it for men too."

"Men I've dated haven't seemed to mind," Mia said reproachfully.

"Yeah, well, for the last time, I'm not a man. Maybe that's the problem." Sydney shrugged.

"Maybe it is," Mia snapped, feeling her anger ignite.

Mia was fairly certain she saw Sydney turn to stone at that point. She knew she'd just said the wrong thing, but she wasn't willing to take it back. It wasn't fair that Sydney had now decided she didn't like

161

what Mia did for a living. She'd known it when they'd gotten together, and she'd been okay with it then. What was she supposed to do? Just quit? She made decent money dancing—it paid her rent and for a few other things like food, electricity and cable.

"Not everyone has a master's degree from Stanford, Syd," Mia said.

"What the fuck does my degree have to do with this conversation?" Sydney asked, her tone sharper than Mia had ever heard it. "What, no man you've ever dated had a degree in anything but chauvinism?"

"Actually, no, no man I've ever known has had a degree in anything. I'm just white trash, I guess," Mia said defensively.

"Where the fuck did that come from?" Sydney asked, glancing sharply at her.

"It's what you think, isn't it?" Mia folded her arms in front of her chest.

Sydney opened her mouth to answer, and then closed it, not sure what to say. She had no idea why Mia thought that, but she also didn't begin to know how to counter it. She pulled up to the apartments, and before she could blink, Mia was out of the car and walking away. Sydney jumped out of the car, watching Mia go.

"Mia!" Sydney called, but Mia simply shook her head and kept walking.

Sydney stood staring after her, watching until Mia got to her apartment, fortunately within view of where Sydney was parked. She waited for Mia to go inside, noting that she slammed the door, then she got back into her car. Driving away, Sydney still couldn't figure out how the evening had suddenly gotten away from her.

She ended up at the Club, sitting off in a corner alone and drinking. It wasn't long before Memphis, who was DJing that night, called the rest of the Lost Bois, who subsequently showed up to drink with Sydney.

"Okay, what do you think happened?" Dakota asked, not for the first time.

"I don't know," Sydney said, shaking her head. "One minute we were talking about her job and the next she's saying I think she's white trash…"

"And who said the thing about maybe you not being a man is the problem?" Dakota asked.

"I think I did, but she agreed to it."

Dakota and Cody rolled their eyes at each other; that was a non-point. They knew fiery women, and Mia's agreeing was just her being pissed off.

"But she brought up your degree?" Harley asked.

Sydney nodded, doing the shot Jet had handed her as she walked up.

"You didn't say anything about your degree first?" Talon asked, also doing the shot in front of her.

"Nope," Sydney said miserably.

"We'll figure this out, Syd," Skyler said, feeling bad for the girl.

"Yeah, we will," Jet agreed.

"Okay, what do we know?" Memphis asked as she walked up on her break.

"Mia's pissed at Syd, and we're trying to figure out why," Kit said.

"Syd, do you know if Mia's talked to her family recently?" Cody asked.

Sydney shrugged. "Got me."

"What are you thinking?" Skyler asked Cody.

"I think she's projecting," Cody said.

"Huh?" Sydney queried, her eyes rather glassy.

163

"Projecting," Cody repeated. "It means that it's what she thinks of herself, and rather than admit that to herself and deal with it, she's projecting on to you, saying that it's what you think of her. It's a coping mechanism." She picked up her beer and took a drink. "My bet would be she talked to her parents or someone from home, and they made her feel bad for her life choices. Or it could just be that she's really unhappy with her life right now, and it's easier to take it out on you than face that reality."

"Thank you, Doctor Falco," Jet said, winking at Cody, "for that fine and rather forensic analysis of this mess."

"You'll get my bill," Cody said, grinning.

"So what does that mean? And what the hell can I do about any of that?" Sydney asked, sounding very drunk.

"It basically means that your girl feels like shit about herself," Skyler said.

"And it's your job to make her feel better," Talon added.

"Fast," Harley said.

"How?" Sydney asked plaintively.

"Depends on how you feel about the girl," Jet said.

"What do you mean?" Sydney asked.

"Jet went all the way to Iraq to save Fadi," Skyler said.

"Sky rescued Devin from a mudslide," Jet said.

Dakota smiled softly. "Jaz rescued me."

"McKenna loved me even though I had her under investigation," Cody said.

Harley grinned. "Shy puts up with my ADHD ass constantly."

"Gage rescued me from my ex-husband holding a knife to my throat," Kit said.

"Kier stayed with me through hell," Memphis said.

"Parker has to put up with fans all the time," Talon said.

Sydney looked at each of her friends, realizing again what amazing people they all were. She started to nod, understanding what they were saying.

The next day, Sydney was at Mia's door by noon. She'd have been there sooner, but she'd needed to get a handle on the killer hangover she had first. In her hands she held purple lilies, Mia's favorite.

When Mia opened the door, it was the first thing she saw, two dozen of the most beautiful purple lilies she'd ever seen. She'd tossed and turned all night, feeling horrible what for had happened with Sydney.

"They're beautiful," Mia said, her blue eyes widening, then she looked up at Sydney.

She could see immediately that Sydney was hungover—it meant she'd had a lot to drink the night before, and it would have had to have been after she'd left Mia's apartment after midnight. Without another word, Mia took Sydney's hand and led her to the couch. Sitting down, she held on to Sydney's hand. She laid the flowers aside and took Sydney's other hand in hers.

"I'm sorry about last night," Mia said. "You rescued me, and I was being a bitch…"

Sydney shook her head. "Your job has been bugging me for a while now, and it's not your fault—it was how I met you. I just… I guess I didn't really know how it was going to make me feel."

"And how do you feel?"

"I hate it, Mia… The idea of some guy, or even another woman, touching you, even if it doesn't mean anything to you…" She shook her head again. "It's still… it's still happening… and… they think… and they… I just can't handle it," she said finally. "I'm sorry, I can't."

Mia nodded, looking like she was trying to understand what Sydney was saying.

"Are you saying you don't want to see me anymore?" Mia asked.

"No!" Sydney said vehemently. "I just... I want you to do something else."

"Something else?" Mia asked, her look pointed.

Sydney swallowed, nodding, seeming hesitant suddenly.

"Like what?" Mia asked suspiciously. "'Cause I don't think flipping burgers or asking 'do you want fries with that?' will make enough to cover my rent."

"What about college?" Sydney asked.

Mia looked back at her like she'd lost her mind. "College costs money, Syd. If I can't pay my rent, how am I supposed to pay for college?"

"So what about you move in with me?" Sydney asked.

Mia's mouth dropped open at the invitation. "Are you serious?"

"Yeah," Sydney said.

"Syd, we've only been dating for like three weeks."

"I know."

"And you just want me to move in?"

Sydney grinned. "You obviously haven't heard the joke about what lesbians bring on a second date..."

"What?"

"U-Haul."

"But that's a joke, right?" Mia asked.

"Based completely in fact. Lesbians move at the speed of light at times."

"Okay, let's say I do that," Mia said. "If I don't have a job, how am I paying for college?"

"Well, there's the Board of Governors waiver for tuition, and I can help with stuff like books."

"No." Mia shook her head. "If I do this, and move in with you, I need to pay half the rent and pay for books and stuff too."

"My rent is three thousand a month."

Mia's eyes widened significantly. "Okay, so I can't afford half your rent even with a job. See? I can't... that's just crazy... You pay three thousand a month?"

Sydney nodded. "Okay, how about this? You move in, and I help you get a student job with the state, maybe even OES, to help with books and stuff."

"And rent?"

"Give me a break here, will ya?" Sydney said.

"Syd, I don't want anyone to support me."

"Everybody needs help sometime."

"That might be true but—"

Sydney's lips on hers stopped whatever she was going to say. The sudden heat throughout her body kept her from thinking for the next few hours. She pushed Sydney back on the couch in her sudden need; Sydney happily accommodated, pulling Mia down with her as her hands made quick work of the tank top and shorts that Mia wore.

They made love on the couch, and again in Mia's bed. They lay together afterwards, with Mia lying over Sydney. Sydney reached up, kissing Mia over and over again and holding her close.

"Will you please let me do this?" Sydney asked beseechingly.

Mia looked down at Sydney. "Why do you want to do this?"

"Because I'm the one saying I can't handle your job, so I should be the one to come up with the solution."

"And just breaking up with me and moving on isn't an option?" Mia asked.

Sydney looked back at her seriously. "Is that what you want me to do?"

Mia's blue eyes searched Sydney's; she could see that Sydney was purposely keeping her expression blank. Finally she shook her head.

"No, I love being with you. But I feel like you think this is the only option."

"I don't think this is the only option, but it's the one I want the most," Sydney said, her smile shy.

"Why?" Mia asked softly.

"Because I want you with me," Sydney said, her voice so earnest that Mia couldn't even begin to imagine saying no to that.

"Okay," Mia said. "But you're going to show me how I can get that student job thing. I don't want you paying for everything."

Sydney's smile would have lit up New York as she nodded.

***

Harley woke late on Sunday morning, hungover from the night before with Sydney and the Lost Bois' rescue mission. Getting up, she immediately went to take a shower, feeling like her body was rebelling in the worst way. After her shower, she felt more human, so she made her way downstairs. Shiloh was nowhere to be found. Harley found a note on the refrigerator that said she'd gone out to lunch with "a friend." It struck Harley as odd, because all of Shiloh's friends were basically Harley's friends too.

Walking back upstairs, she checked her phone: no texts. She texted the bois asking if Shiloh was having lunch with any of their girls; she got back all negatives. It was later in the afternoon when Sydney responded, asking what was going on. Harley texted back that Shiloh was hanging out with a friend, and she had just been curious which of their friends she was hanging out with and not to worry about it.

"Jesus, Harl…" Sydney muttered.

"What's up?" Mia asked. They were packing up Mia's apartment.

Sydney sighed. "There might be a problem."

"What kind of problem?" Mia asked, sitting down next to Sydney on her bed.

"Harley's girl is maybe seeing some guy behind Harley's back… then again, probably right in Harley's face, and my girl just doesn't see it," she said, shaking her head ruefully.

It was five o'clock by the time Shiloh showed back up at the house. Harley was deeply involved with a computer program by that time. It took until that night as they were getting into bed for Harley to ask, "So who'd you have lunch with anyway?"

Shiloh paused, then shrugged. "Just a friend."

Harley nodded. In bed, she pulled Shiloh to her to kiss her goodnight—that was when she caught the scent of cologne. She angled her head down at Shiloh.

"Is that cologne?" Harley's tone was far from accusatory, but that wasn't the way Shiloh heard it.

"What's that supposed to mean?" Shiloh said, turning over to look at Harley.

Harley's blue eyes widened. "It was just a question."

"You come home smelling like Sydney half the time," Shiloh retorted. "I don't accuse you of anything."

Harley stared at Shiloh like she couldn't fathom what Shiloh meant.

"I mean, you had to leave our bed last night at midnight to go rescue her, right?" Shiloh went on.

"She was upset," Harley said by way of explanation.

"Yeah, I know," Shiloh said derisively. "She needed you."

"Us, it was all of us."

"Right," Shiloh said, rolling her eyes.

"Okay, what's going on?" Harley didn't like the way Shiloh was acting; it was very unlike her.

"I think I'm really starting to see why other women had a problem with you."

Harley blinked as if Shiloh had actually slapped her. She got out of bed and stood looking down at Shiloh. Shiloh had turned her back to Harley and didn't turn to see Harley looking at her. She heard the door to the bedroom close quietly.

Harley never came back to bed. Shiloh fell into a fitful sleep, waking every hour or so and noting that Harley wasn't in bed. She refused to get up and go look for her.

Harley showed up at Sydney's apartment at ten thirty. Sydney opened the door, surprised.

"What's going on?" Sydney asked as Harley walked inside looking absolutely morose.

"You were right; she's cheating on me," Harley said, her tone completely defeated.

Sydney followed Harley into the living room and out to the patio. where Harley had gone to smoke. She glanced over at Mia, who'd come out of the bedroom to see who had been at the door. Sydney shook her head. She'd told Mia about Harley and how she felt like Shiloh was getting pulled away by this guy from a local fire department and that Harley wasn't seeing it. Now it seemed that she had been right. She hated being right this time.

Sydney walked out to the terrace and leaned against the railing, looking over at Harley.

"Did she tell you that?" Sydney asked mildly.

"She doesn't have to," Harley said. "She was out to lunch with someone all day, didn't come home till like five… and when I ask who she was at lunch with she says it's a 'friend,'" she said, using air quotes. "Oh, and to top it off, she smells like cologne."

"Okay, so go kick the guy's ass."

"Why?" Harley asked, her voice barely audible.

"Because he's fucking with your girl, Harl, why else!"

"She had to give him the invitation," Harley said, shrugging and shaking her head. "He just took her up on it."

"And that's okay with you?" Sydney asked hotly.

Harley blinked slowly and finished her cigarette, and then looked over at Sydney.

"Okay if I crash in your office?" she asked.

"Uh, yeah, sure," Sydney said, confused by the shift in subjects.

Harley nodded, pushing off the railing and heading inside. Sydney watched her go. She knew something had just shifted in Harley, and she wasn't sure she liked it. Going into her own room, she picked up her phone and texted Devin. Devin knew Harley the best out of everyone.

SYD: *Harley just showed up at my place. She thinks Shy is cheating on her with a guy from work. Seems like she's done… What do I do?"*

DEVIN: *A guy from work?*

SYD: *Yeah some firefighter.*

DEVIN: *She's done? What did she say?*

SYD: *I asked her if she was going to kick the guy's ass, she asked why.*

DEVIN: *Yeah… that's classic Harley. She's giving up.*

SYD: On Shiloh????

DEVIN: Yep, she doesn't fight for women. Too many women have confounded her over the years.

SYD: So she'll just give up?

DEVIN: It used to happen a lot, Shy lasted longer than most.

At Devin and Skyler's house, Skyler had just gotten into bed when Devin's phone chimed. She noted Devin shaking her head.

"What's up?" Skyler asked her wife.

"Harley's at Syd's apartment. She says Shy is cheating on her with a guy."

"What?" Skyler practically yelled. "How does she know this?"

"I don't know," Devin said. "But Syd's pretty sure she knows who it is."

"So when do we kick the guy's ass?"

"We?" Devin asked mildly.

"Mess with one Lost Boi, you get us all," Skyler said with a wintery smile.

"Oh, my…" Devin said. "Well, the bad news is that Harley seems to be letting this one go."

"Are you fucking kidding me?" Skyler asked, reaching for her phone. "Tell Syd I'm going to text her."

Devin grinned. "Okay."

SKYLER: Where is Harley?

SYD: She's crashing in my office, why?

SKYLER: Because we're not putting up with this shit. Who is this guy?

SYD: He's a firefighter with LAFD.

SKYLER: What's his name?

SYD: Garcia I think.

SKYLER: *Fucker! I know him, he's a piece of work.*

SYD: *You know him? How?*

SKYLER: *I used to work for LA Fire, Syd.*

SYD: *Oh good to know.*

SKYLER: *We're not letting him get away with this.*

SYD: *Harley doesn't seem interested in fighting for Shy.*

SKYLER: *Then you're going to have to convince her.*

SYD: *How?*

SKYLER: *Be creative. Call me when you've woken her ass up.*

Skyler put her phone back on the nightstand and looked over at Devin; Devin was still texting. Skyler grinned.

"Let me guess—she's asking you how to do what I just told her to do?" Skyler asked.

Devin smirked as she continued to text, her expression becoming particularly evil. As she finished texting, she looked at her wife.

"Fightin' a little fire with fire, babe." Devin winked.

"Oh lord," Skyler said.

The next morning when the alarm went off, Shiloh got up and noted that Harley still wasn't in bed. She took a shower and got ready for work. She went looking for Harley, only to find that Harley wasn't there. She checked the garage, and the Z wasn't there. Shiloh texted Gage to tell her that she would be in late that day and that she didn't know for sure if Harley would be in or not.

Gage texted back asking what was wrong. Shiloh replied that she wasn't sure.

Sydney walked into her office the next morning to see that Harley was lying facedown on the futon that she'd laid out. Harley had taken the time to kick off her tennis shoes and shrug out of her jacket, but she hadn't bothered with anything else. Sydney knew Harley was awake because her foot was bouncing in agitation, a sign that her ADHD was in hyperdrive.

Sitting down next to her friend, Sydney slid her hand over Harley's back.

"How ya doing?" she asked.

"Fine," Harley said, her voice almost as mechanical as her answer.

Sydney nodded. Lying down next to Harley, she put her chin on Harley's shoulder.

"I'm sorry, this sucks," Sydney said.

"How did things go with Mia?" Harley mumbled, her voice muffled because it was still half buried in the pillow under her head.

"Eh, you know," Sydney said non-committally.

Harley turned over then, looking at Sydney. "She'll come around."

"Maybe it won't matter," Sydney said, her tone insinuating.

Harley looked confused. "Why wouldn't it matter?"

Sydney slid her hand over Harley's arm seductively. "Well, you're here now," she said with a sly grin.

"So?" Harley said, still looking lost.

"So maybe it's time you and I give it a go." Sydney leaned up over Harley, staring down at her.

"Uh, Syd…"

Without warning, Sydney kissed Harley on the lips, pressing against her. Harley's hands shot out to her sides, and then up to Sydney's shoulders to push her away as she all but ripped her lips away from Sydney's.

"Harley?" Sydney queried, with just the right amount of hurt and confusion.

"Sydney, no," Harley said, shaking her head. "Jesus, I'm in love with Shiloh. I can't do this with you. I love ya, Syd, I really do, but not like that."

Sydney grinned.

"You love Shiloh?" Sydney asked, reaching out to touch Harley again.

"Yes!" Harley said as she stood up quickly to get away from Sydney's hands.

"Good!" Sydney said, standing up too. "Then go and fucking fight for her."

"What?" Harley asked, blinking in confusion.

"I'm not into you, Harl, never was, but I needed you to remember that you're in love with Shiloh. You can't just give her up, not like before. Fight for her."

Harley stared at Sydney, and a slow smile spread over her face, her blue eyes sparkling in the morning sunlight.

Shiloh was at work. Harley had not come into the office, nor had she called, according to Gage. Shiloh was starting to worry. She'd texted all of the Lost Bois and their friends asking if they'd seen her. No one had. She was about to start calling CHP and hospitals and was just picking up the phone when John Garcia walked up to her desk.

He was all smiles; they'd had a nice lunch the day before. Even though she'd refused to go back to his place with him, he was sure it was just a matter of time. She was really a hot piece, and he was dying to see what kind of nasty sex they'd have. As it was, he had a hard-on all the time for her because of her sexy lesbo boss. Just picturing the two together got him hot.

"Not right now, John, okay?" Shiloh said, shaking her head.

"What's wrong? Can I help?"

"No, nothing," Shiloh said. "It's fine."

"Oh, come on, let me help..." he said in what he considered his most charming voice.

"I think she said no," Gage said from behind John. "Isn't that what you heard, Kit?"

"Oh yes," Kit said, nodding.

"She definitely said no," Jocelyn agreed from the doorway to John's left.

"Sounded like no to me," Sebastian said, standing with his legs apart and his arms crossed over his chest.

"Yeah, it definitely sounded like no to me too," Kashena said.

Shenin leaned against Shiloh's desk. "Yeah, that's clearly how I heard it too."

John looked around at all the faces of the various deputy directors, the executive deputy director and the director of OES. He decided he might just want to move on this morning. Holding up his hands, he stepped back from Shiloh's desk.

"Sorry," he said, smiling. "I'll get out of your way," he said to Shiloh.

John turned and almost ran into Harley, who stood firmly in his path. She looked even less like a deputy director than she did normally. Today she wore a black tank top with a tooled black leather Harley-Davidson jacket, black skinny jeans and black combat boots. She wore black dog tags around her neck and a fairly nasty expression on her face.

"You and I need to talk," Harley said, her blue eyes glinting with barely contained malice.

"Harley..." Shiloh said from her desk.

Harley held her hand out to Shiloh in a halting movement, her gaze not wavering from John.

"You want to do this here or outside?" Harley asked, looking every bit the biker at that moment.

John glanced around at the other directors and saw that none of them appeared shocked by Harley's behavior. Finally he nodded. "Let's go outside."

Turning on her heel, Harley led the way out of the building. Shiloh jumped up from her desk and followed the two. She'd never seen Harley like this, and she wasn't sure what that meant. Gage, Kit, Jocelyn, Sebastian, Kashena and Shenin followed.

Harley walked out the front doors, as did John, and he was stunned by what he saw.

Very butch, very angry-looking women were ranged around the entrance, on motorcycles and leaning against muscle cars.

Harley grinned. Not only were all of the Lost Bois there, but so were all of the other butches in the group. Ty, Quinn, Lyric and all of the Lost Bois except Talon were on their bikes; Cat, Jericho and Rayden all leaned against Jericho's Challenger Hellcat; Remington and Kai leaned against Kai's green Mercedes-AMG; Sinclair, Parker and Talon leaned against Parker's Cougar; and Legend sat on the hood of her 'Cuda. They all had dangerous looks on their faces.

Jet, Skyler, Dakota, Sydney and Cody stood in front of John to stop him from continuing to walk. John stared at the various women, thinking remotely that they were all fairly hot, but noting that they all looked like they'd happily kill him if he even thought about it for long. Kai and Remington walked up with Jericho and Rayden, and they were a little more formidable looking.

John turned to Harley, who looked back at him with a nasty smirk.

"You've been messing with something that belongs to me," Harley said. "And today it stops."

"Hey, she didn't seem to mind," John said, holding up his hands coolly.

"I mind," Harley said in a low growl. "And that's what you need to know."

"And what are you going to do?" John asked.

Harley canted her head at Remington, who walked over to John and clamped her hand around his throat, turning him and backing him up against Kai.

"I was a Marine for eight years. Kai, you got fourteen, right?" Remington said.

"Yep," Kai said, her dark eyes flashing.

"So you think that either one of us couldn't take your ass apart?" Remington asked.

"Plus Remi was an MMA fighter," Jericho added from John's right.

"You ever see her fight?" Rayden asked.

"She could turn your ass to mush, Garcia, count on it," Skyler said from the side.

"Boché! Hey, tell them I'm just a flirt. I don't mean any harm," John said.

"Right, sure you don't," Skyler said, narrowing her light blue-green eyes.

"You need to stay away from my girl," Harley told John as Remington released him and stepped back. "Am I making myself clear?"

"Yeah, yeah, or you'll sic your friends on me," John said, pulling out his last shred of manhood.

"I don't need my friends to kick your ass," Harley said evenly. "They just wanted to come support me. That's how us lesbos are."

John looked Harley up and down, a sneer on his face. Harley saw Remington and Kai start to step forward, but she held out her hand to stop them. She tilted her head, and Shiloh, who'd been watching from the semicircle of directors, knew what was about to happen. She saw one tiny little flex on Harley's part before she threw a punch that downed John instantly.

"Bangarang!" Jet crowed.

"Bangarang!" the rest of the group replied.

Shiloh heard Sebastian mutter, "Son of a bitch…"

Harley had turned and was striding toward Shiloh. Taking her into her arms, Harley kissed her deeply, so deeply, in fact, that Shiloh completely forgot that they were standing in front of the office and wrapped her arms around Harley's neck, kissing her back.

The catcalls started. Harley stepped back, keeping her arms around Shiloh and gazing down at her earnestly.

"I love you. I'm sorry I let you forget that." Her blue eyes searched Shiloh's. "It will never happen again."

Shiloh smiled up at Harley, putting her hand to Harley's cheek.

"I love you too, and I promise I won't lose sight of that again… Should I even look at your hand at this point?"

"It hurts like hell," Harley said, grinning.

"I figured."

Harley turned, her arm around Shiloh, and walked over to everyone. She thanked them for being there for her.

"That's what friends do, Harl," Skyler said. "Nice punch."

"Learned that from Remi."

"And you did good," Remington said. "Nice and loose. Not that he was responding or anything."

"Best kind of punch," Kai put in with a grin.

The next morning, Shenin woke to the sensation of her neck being touched. She stirred and opened her eyes. Tyler was awake and looking down at her, but not at her as much as at her neck. She felt Tyler's finger brush over a sore spot.

"What is this?" Tyler asked evenly.

"You tell me," Shenin said, smiling. "I can't see it."

"Looks like a scratch."

Shenin looked contemplative.

"Oh, yeah... yesterday I was talking to a battalion chief about how I wanted him to set the plan to load one of my C27s. Oh my God, that man is dense! He refused to listen to me, because what does a little girlie director know about loading a C27. Ugh! Anyway, I was wearing my headset while I was talking to him—Kimber got me one of those wireless ones so I could pace while I talk. I got so mad I yanked it off my neck, and I must have scratched myself in the process. I was so pissed I didn't even notice."

Tyler nodded, her look indicating that she wasn't sure she believed her.

"What, you thought it was a hickey or something?" Shenin asked, grinning.

Tyler's expression changed slightly, and Shenin saw that it was exactly what Tyler thought.

"Jesus, Ty." Shenin shook her head as she sat up. "You thought it was a hickey..."

"You worked late again last night," Tyler said.

"Because we're having wildfires go off everywhere. It's a logistics nightmare and I'm trying to make sure we cover everyone."

Shenin could see she wasn't getting through. When Tyler decided something it took an act of God to get her to change her mind. Getting out of bed, Shenin pulled on her pajamas, her movements angry.

Tyler watched, dreading what was coming next. Shenin completely shocked her by sitting down on the bed again, facing her. Tyler had expected her to leave the room.

"This has to stop, Ty," Shenin said, her tone serious.

"What does?" Tyler asked warily.

"That!" Shenin exclaimed sharply. "You waiting for the other shoe to drop. There is no other shoe, why don't you get that?"

Tyler didn't answer, but it was clear in her eyes that she didn't believe Shenin. In desperation, Shenin straddled Tyler's waist, taking Tyler's face in her hands.

"Tyler, you are the only woman I have ever wanted. Nothing and no one is ever going to change that. But this off-the-chain jealousy that has you imagining things about me and someone else has just got to stop, because it's going to kill us like no man or woman could. Don't you see that?"

Tyler looked back at her, and Shenin could see that she desperately wanted to believe her.

"Have I ever given you a reason to not trust me?" Shenin asked. "Have I ever cheated on you?"

Tyler swallowed, shaking her head.

"No," Shenin said, "and I never will, Tyler. I love you and I love what we have, but you're driving me crazy with this shit." She smiled to take the bite out of her words. "Remember when you were sure about Jet and Skyler being after me? Remember how wrong you were?"

Tyler grimaced, nodding.

181

When they had been separated by an entire country, with Tyler back in Washington, DC, and Shenin in Los Angeles, Tyler had been dismayed to hear that two butch women had befriended Shenin. She was further distressed when she met Jet and Skyler and found out how extremely good-looking they were. In the end, she found out that they were good friends to Shenin. It had been Skyler who'd saved Shenin's life when she'd given in to the demons that lived inside of her and tried to kill herself. Jet and Skyler had turned out to be nothing like Tyler had imagined, and she'd felt incredibly stupid to have thought that way.

"Well, babe, this is another case of that," Shenin said, holding up her hand. "I will admit that Kimber has been dropping little come-ons here and there, and I'll also admit that it's been nice to hear, but not once did I consider taking her up on any of them. Okay?"

Tyler's eyes narrowed. "She's been coming on to you?" she asked darkly.

"Oh my God, is that the only thing you heard?" Shenin exclaimed.

Tyler grinned. "No, baby, it isn't. And you're right, I need to get a handle on the jealousy thing. I'm sorry."

Tyler touched Shenin's cheek. Shenin leaned in and kissed her. Tyler's hands slid around her back, pulling Shenin closer as she deepened the kiss. Shenin slid her hands up Tyler's chest, caressing and pressing closer. Tyler removed the pajamas that Shenin had just put on, laid her back on the bed, and took her time to make love to her, reminding Shenin over and over again why they were so well matched sexually.

Afterwards, Shenin reciprocated, making herself late for work but happy to remind her wife what they had together. When Shenin finally got up to shower for work, she was surprised when Tyler joined her in the shower.

"Where are you going?" Shenin asked her wife.

"With you to work," Tyler said, her blue eyes twinkling mischievously.

"What about Aiden?"

"Jenny's here," Tyler told her.

"How…" Shenin asked.

"I planned on going in with you today anyway," Tyler said. "I planned on setting your little secretary straight about who you belonged to. Now I know that I don't have to actually kill her…" Her voice trailed off with barely veiled malice.

"Tyler, I don't want to have to quit my job today, okay?"

Tyler waggled her eyebrows.

Later as Shenin was getting ready, she walked into their bedroom and noticed that Tyler was dressing way more butch than she usually did. She was wearing jeans, Harley-Davidson boots, and a black USAF Security Forces T-shirt with a picture of a skull with a beret on and crossed M16s. On top of that she wore her Harley-Davidson leathers, chaps and jacket.

Shenin raised an eyebrow at her wife. "I take it you're riding your Harley down?"

"Uh-huh," Tyler said, looking amused.

Shenin looked at her wife for a moment, then shook her head. "You're gonna get me fired. I can feel it!"

"No," Tyler said. "But I am going to make sure that little girl knows who you belong to and not to fuck with that ever again."

"Ty, I can tell her not to say anything else; you don't need to do this," Shenin said, truly worried that her very passionate, fairly strong wife was going to damage her secretary.

Tyler walked over to Shenin, taking her by the shoulders. "Okay, let's say that some woman at the base was coming on to me and I told you about it, but said I'd handle it. What would you do?"

Shenin pursed her lips in thought. "Okay yeah, I'd want to confront her myself, you're right, but I'm not near as dangerous as you are, Ty. I need you to not damage her, okay?"

"That'll depend on her."

Two hours later, Tyler had made the rounds, talking to the girls and Sebastian. Kimber was sitting at her desk and had no idea that Tyler was there. So she was very surprised when Tyler walked up and glared down at her.

Kimber looked up into Tyler's very blue eyes and noted the very butch-looking outfit and the fact that her long curly hair was pulled back into a braid down her back.

"Do you have a minute?" Tyler asked Kimber pleasantly.

"Sure," Kimber said, standing up.

Tyler gestured to Shenin's office, so Kimber walked inside. Shenin looked up from her desk. She didn't say a word; she just watched what happened next.

Tyler walked over to Shenin's desk, turning her back to Shenin and leaning against the edge, her eyes on Kimber.

"So," Tyler said, her face serious. "I understand you've been coming on to my wife."

"I, no, I mean…" Kimber stammered.

"Yeah, that wasn't a question," Tyler said, her blue eyes narrowed. "If my wife says you're coming on to her, you are. What you and I are about to do is talk about what we're going to do about that."

Kimber stared at Tyler, swallowing convulsively.

"Now, what I'd like to do is beat the living shit out of you for even considering messing with my marriage and my wife," Tyler said, her tone low. "Shenin says I'm not allowed to do that... but you need to know that I don't always do what my wife tells me."

Kimber's eyes widened, then she nodded slowly, her gaze going to Shenin.

"No," Tyler said. "Don't look at her. She's not going to help you at this point. Do you know why?"

"Why?" Kimber asked tremulously.

"Because she loves me more than she cares to protect your ass, that's why. And do you know why she loves me?"

Kimber shook her head.

"Because we've been through a lot of shit together and we've come out the other side. And she knows that I will protect her and what we have together with my life, so she's never going to give me up for someone like you."

Tyler stood from the desk and took a few surprisingly long strides toward Kimber, backing the girl up against the door. Tyler stood a good four inches taller than Kimber, and was far more intimidating than Kimber could ever even dream of being. Tyler stared down at the girl, her hands on the door at either side of Kimber's head, her blue eyes practically shooting sparks of anger.

"If you ever fuck with my wife again," Tyler said, her voice a low growl, "I will not hesitate to rip your throat out, do you understand me?" She was all security force at that moment, and Shenin couldn't help but feel pretty damned proud of her wife. The woman had incredibly sexy, intense command presence in spades.

Kimber nodded slowly, feeling the very definite threat from Tyler Hancock's closeness. The woman was downright scary. Kimber hadn't imagined that someone who looked like Tyler could be intimidating—she was wrong. Tyler reached behind Kimber and opened the door for her, then gestured for her to leave. Kimber did, in a hurry.

Tyler closed the door behind her and turned around in time to meet her wife coming toward her.

"Have I mentioned how hot you are when you're all butch like that?" Shenin asked, grinning.

"No, do tell…" Tyler said, smiling as she leaned in to kiss her.

Shenin pressed closer, locking her office door. "How about I show you instead of telling you?"

Tyler answered by sliding her hand around the back of Shenin's neck, pulling her to her to kiss her deeply. They did their best to be quiet, but Kimber definitely heard them and grinned, shaking her head. She'd definitely learned her lesson there, but damn if Tyler Hancock wasn't hotter than hell if she could make Shenin that happy.

***

Sable walked into the master bedroom to see that Jocelyn was on the phone. She stood in the doorway, gazing at the woman she was in love with. It was still so hard to believe that Jocelyn loved her too. Sable had been through so much before, falling for Catalina Roché even when Catalina was still in love with someone else, only to lose her to yet another woman. It was impossible to truly believe that Jocelyn really loved her and wasn't going to change her mind.

It had been five months since they'd gotten back together. Jocelyn had completed chemotherapy, and the last round had gone extremely well. With everyone keeping an eye on her and helping her with various supplements and tips, Jocelyn had not only actually managed to put weight back on, but she'd been training with Kai to add to her strength and stamina.

Sable's eyes moved over Jocelyn, who was sitting with her back to the headboard of the bed, one long leg extended out in front of her, her other foot up on the bed. She was wearing jeans and a shirt with "United States Army Aviation" and the wings and rotor blade on the front, and, as usual, black cowboy boots. She was still as slim as ever, but there was very definite muscle in her thighs. Sable felt herself shiver at the thought of what lay under those clothes.

With that thought in mind, Sable climbed onto the bed, putting her head on Jocelyn's extended leg, facing up at Jocelyn, who smiled at her.

"I'm on hold," Jocelyn told her, as her hand reached out to touch Sable's face, then slid into her hair. "Yes, I'm still here," she said into the phone a minute later. "Okay…" she said then, looking serious. "Okay… So what does that mean?" She nodded, glancing down at Sable, her dark eyes unreadable. "Okay, thank you." She hung up the phone.

"Who was that?" Sable asked.

"My doctor."

Sable sat up; she knew they'd done scans earlier that day, but she hadn't expected any results this fast. Her face was fearful as she looked at Jocelyn.

"What did they say?" Sable asked.

"They said that at this point everything is clear."

"Okay… That's good, right?"

"Right," Jocelyn said. "He said that I need to go in every twelve weeks for check-ups and retesting, because if it comes back we want to catch it early. But for now… we're in the clear."

"Then why don't you seem happy?" Sable asked worriedly.

Jocelyn looked pensive. "I guess I'm not really sure how I feel about the cancer. Part of me didn't want to think past this moment when they'd say live or die."

Sable put her head against Jocelyn's chest. Jocelyn's arms wrapped around her, pulling her close as she kissed the top of Sable's head.

"I couldn't have done this without you," she said softly. "I hope you know that."

Sable turned her face up toward Jocelyn. "I'm just glad you let me help you. You were incredibly brave through this."

Jocelyn's look flickered, which showed she doubted that, but she kissed Sable gently. When their lips parted, Jocelyn grinned.

"I kind of did something a couple of weeks ago... just in case."

"In case of what?" Sable asked, looking worried.

"Well, good news." Jocelyn opened her nightstand drawer and took out a small box. She held it up to Sable.

"What is that?" Sable asked, not daring to hope.

Jocelyn smiled. "Open it."

Sable opened the box to see the most beautiful ring—two rows of pavé-set chocolate diamonds with a third row of vanilla diamonds in the center, swirling into a large oval burgundy solitaire, set in rose gold.

"Jocelyn, it's beautiful..." she breathed, biting her lip and trying not to cry.

"Will you marry me?" Jocelyn asked earnestly.

Sable looked up at Jocelyn, her eyes glazed with unshed tears. In Jocelyn's eyes she saw the love she'd been craving for years. She couldn't believe that she'd found it in the last place she would have ever looked, in a butch woman... Sometimes you just had to look in a different way, she guessed.

"I'm not getting an answer here…" Jocelyn said, smiling.

"Of course I'll marry you!" Sable said with a laugh. "How could I not?"

"That means you'll need to stay here in LA, you know."

"Well, you could come to London with me to see how you like it…" Sable said.

"Who says I've never been to London?"

"Have you?"

"No," Jocelyn said, grinning, "but we can definitely go there."

"But we live here," Sable said, saying the words Jocelyn didn't.

"Right."

Sable nodded. "Jake likes it here."

"Well, there ya go." Jocelyn said, laughing.

Chapter 8

"I don't know if I can get resources there!" Shenin yelled out to Kimber. "See if Cal Fire's got anything left at their Hemet air attack base!"

"On it!" Kimber called back.

"Jesus, it's getting dark out there," Sebastian said as he strode into Shenin's office. "What have you got for me?"

Shenin handed him a sheaf of papers. "It's not great, but it'll have to do."

Sebastian looked the papers over, his eyes scanning the numbers.

"Jesus Christ, seriously?" he asked. "Is literally all of California on fire?"

"Pretty much," Kimber said as she walked into Shenin's office, handing her the latest reports.

"Goddamn it! I thought we got retardant sent here too!" Shenin said.

"Nope, it never got here," Kimber said. "I'm trying to track it down right now. But they're running out."

"Great, so the OES office is going to crash and burn because we didn't get fire retardant sent to our area?" Shenin asked wryly.

"Well, that's a lousy attitude," Jocelyn said as she walked into Shenin's office, passing Sebastian, who looked harried.

"Sorry, Gun, it's the only one I have right now," Shenin said, smiling all the same. "What's up?"

"I got Temecula screaming that they're running out of retardant too."

"Check?" Shenin asked Kimber as her phone rang again.

Kimber nodded and went back to her desk to pull up the information.

When Shenin got off the phone, she looked at Jocelyn. "How are you feeling?"

"All good," Jocelyn said, grinning.

Everyone had heard Jocelyn's news and had been ecstatic about both the general all-clear on the cancer and about Sable and Jocelyn getting married. The wedding was planned for Christmas in Mendocino; they were hoping to keep it low key, hence the remote location. Also, Jocelyn had spent a lot of time there when she'd lived in San Francisco—she loved the area.

"Good," Shenin said.

"So it's looking like I better tell Harley that we might want to start exporting offsite for our data?" Jocelyn asked seriously.

"Might not be a bad idea," Shenin said. "Will you brief Gage?"

"Yeah, I'm meeting up with her in a few at the copter. I'll talk to her then," Jocelyn said with a wink.

They'd finally gotten the helicopter they'd been asking for—a Sikorsky Firehawk that had been gifted to them from the California Department of Forestry and Fire Protection, known as Cal Fire. Gage used it to assess areas during emergencies; as always, Jocelyn was her co-pilot.

Twenty minutes later, Jocelyn climbed into the Firehawk. Gage was already working on preflight.

"So we're having issues with retardant getting to our locals," Jocelyn told Gage as she started doing her half of preflight.

"Like, *local* local?" Gage asked, sounding shocked.

"Yeah," Jocelyn said. "I've already told Harley and Syd to start transferring data to the backup site."

"Holy shit," Gage said, shaking her head. "I was really hoping we'd get a handle on this. How's it going to look if the OES gets eaten?"

"It's going to look like we were busy helping everyone else out."

"We ready?" Gage asked as she started the rotors.

"Yep, we're clear."

A minute later the Firehawk lifted off. They had to do a sudden evasive maneuver to avoid one of the helicopters taking off from the Army airfield located nearby.

"Holy fuck!" Gage exclaimed as she made a quick move to avoid a collision. "This is OES N2678," she yelled into the mic. "Hey, Tower, can you keep your people out of my damned airspace? We just had a near collision here."

"Apologies, N2678. Things are getting crazy here."

Gage shook her head at Jocelyn. "We get out of fucking Iraq and get killed in LA? Seriously?"

Jocelyn grinned. "So much fun here... Head forty degrees east," Jocelyn said into her headset. "I want to take a look at the Chino Hills fire to see where we are."

"Got it," Gage said, making the adjustments to head in the direction Jocelyn had said.

They were over the site few minutes later.

"Yeah, that does not look like there's going to be containment anytime soon," Jocelyn said. "Do you see more than three units there?"

"Can't tell. I'm going to get in closer," Gage said.

"Let's not singe our new rotors, huh?"

"Bite me." Gage pushed the copter forward, dropping lower. "I'm seeing three. Shit, they need more units. Call it in, Gun."

"Got it," Jocelyn said, keying the radio and calling it in to Kashena.

"Are you fucking kidding me?" Kashena shouted into the radio. "I sent ten over there! What did the other seven do, go to lunch? Damnit! I'm on it, Gun. We'll get people over there."

"Good, thanks." Jocelyn looked over at Gage. "Want to head over to Santiago?"

"Yeah," Gage said, steering the helicopter in that direction.

Two hours later, the team at OES got word to Gage and Jocelyn that the smoke was getting so bad in the building that they needed to get people out. The building was evacuated of all non-essential staff.

"I've got the generators running, to pull the smoke away from the command room," Shenin told Jocelyn on the radio.

"Okay, make sure you all don't stay in there too long," Jocelyn said. "The fire is moving fast and right now away from the building, but it could shift. I don't want any of you in its path, so start looking at an exit plan for the emergency staff."

"I want them to start shifting operations," Gage told Jocelyn. "If we wait too long it could be too late."

"Got it," Jocelyn said into her mic, then keyed the radio. "Shen, Gage wants you guys to start transitioning the operations to the other site, and then get out of there, okay?"

"Roger that," Shenin said.

An hour later, Shenin was still running around trying to get things shifted to the other site. It wasn't going well.

"What do you mean the server won't come up?" Shenin asked Harley.

"I mean, I can't see it from here—it's not powering up at the other building. I can't transfer data until I can see the damned thing here," Harley said, jabbing her finger at her screen where the errant server should be showing up as active. "I've sent Syd over there to figure out what's going on, but I'm SOL right now, Shen, I'm sorry. We've got to keep operations here for now."

"Damn it!" Shenin said. "I'll let Gage and Gun know."

"I'm trying, Shen, I really am," Harley said, looking apologetic.

"I know," Shenin said, putting her hand on Harley's arm. "Just keep at it, and let me know when you get that server up."

"You got it." Harley strode off.

Shenin turned to Kimber. "Any luck with stealing some retardant?"

"Still working on it. I'm giving it my best charm, I promise," Kimber said, grinning.

"Promise them whatever we have to, just get that shit here!" Shenin said, her voice sharper than she meant it to be. "Sorry, Kimber, that wasn't directed at you."

"I know. Everything is going to hell in a handbasket right now."

"We just need to get stuff where it needs to go," Shenin said.

"I know," Kimber said, going back to her phones and making another call.

Shenin stood watching Kimber work. The girl had really stepped up. She'd also apologized profusely to Shenin after her confrontation with Tyler. She'd told Shenin that she hadn't meant to be disrespectful, but she understood now that even flirting with someone else's lady was not okay and she promised she wouldn't do it again. She'd held true to that promise and had turned out to be one of the best assistants Shenin had ever had.

"Why are you still here?" Tyler asked as she strode up to Shenin.

"Why are you here at all?" Shenin asked. "Where's Aiden?"

"He's fine, he's with Jenny. You need to get out of this building. The fires are all around you now. Haven't you seen how dark it is out there?"

"I can't go yet, Ty. We need to make sure we get retardant to all of these groups," she said, gesturing to the board in her office as she walked back into it.

"I need to make sure my wife is okay. I don't give a crap about anyone else," Tyler said.

"Ty, I'm fine, okay? But we need to do this…"

"I thought you guys had a backup location," Tyler said.

"We do, but the damned servers won't come up. Syd's on her way there to check it out."

"Mia, just get to my parents' house," Sydney was saying as she drove like a bat out of hell to the backup location, even traveling in the emergency lane when she needed to avoid traffic. "The fires over there are out, so you'll be safe there."

"Traffic is insane right now, Syd. I'm just going to stay in the apartment."

"There's all kinds of craziness going on in the city right now, Mia. I don't think it's safe," Sydney said in a worried tone.

"I'll lock the door," Mia joked.

"Babe, I'm dead serious. I don't want you at the apartment."

"Sydney, I don't want to be out there with all the crazy people either. I'll just stay here and wait till you get home, okay?"

"Babe, I don't know when that's going to be," Sydney said. "I'm headed to our backup location to try to figure out why the damned server isn't working. I could be there a while… I don't want anything to happen to you."

"I'll be fine, Syd, don't worry about me," Mia said.

"I'm going to worry about you until I know you're safe, Mia."

Suddenly there was static, and the line went dead. Cell towers had been going down all over the city due to the fires.

"Son of a bitch!" Sydney exclaimed, jamming her foot down on the gas pedal of the Z, thinking if maybe she could get the server fixed she could swing by the apartment to pick up Mia.

She kept having visions of someone breaking into the apartment to loot it and Mia getting hurt, or worse…

An hour later she was ready to throw the server out the nearest window. She and one of the techs onsite were working on it. They had it open and were testing wires. Finally, after a number of tries, the computer server fired to life when they pushed the power button.

"Okay, we're up! Bangarang!" Sydney crowed to Harley.

"Bangarang!" Harley replied, looking at the tech on her end. "Hit it!"

The tech nodded, grinning at the deputy director who'd just quoted the Lost Boys from *Hook*—she was definitely one of a kind. Within minutes the data was transferring.

"Got it!" Sydney said on her end. "Lock it up, and get us up and running," Sydney told the tech.

"Yes, ma'am," the tech said.

"Harl, I'm gonna run by my place and get Mia, okay?" Sydney said.

"Yeah, go," Harley said. "I know you're worried."

"Thanks," Sydney said. "Do you need me back there or do you want me here?"

"I want you there," Harley said. "Grab Mia and head back there, okay?"

"Got it. You and Shy get out of there soon. That smoke is getting thick."

"Will do. Be safe!"

"You too!" Sydney said.

"Okay, time to go," Tyler said as the building's power went out.

"The generator will kick on," Shenin said, as it did just that.

"Shenin, we need to get out of here," Tyler said. "They've evacuated every house within a three-mile radius. We're the only people still in the area."

"I know, but I need to finish this up…"

"No, you need to get up, and both of you need to come with me right now," Tyler said in a no-nonsense tone.

"Ty—"

"Shenin! Now!" Tyler exclaimed, not willing to compromise her wife's safety anymore.

Shenin actually jumped at the timbre of Tyler's voice. She knew it was exactly how she got people to follow her orders.

"Kimber, let's pack it in. We're being escorted out of the building by Security Force here," she said, nodding at Tyler.

Kimber stood up from her desk. "Well, she's probably right."

"We need to make sure everyone is out," Shenin said. "Kimber, you head over to Harley's offices downstairs and make sure she and Shy are out. Ty and I will head up to Gage's offices and check in with Kash and Baz."

"Okay," Kimber said.

"Meet us downstairs. We'll get you home, okay?" Shenin looked at Tyler, who nodded.

"Got it."

Shenin radioed Gage and Jocelyn, telling them that she was doing a final evacuation of the building and that she was going up to Gage's office to get Kit out as well as Baz and Kashena.

"Roger that," Jocelyn said. "Thanks. Be careful!"

"You too!" Shenin called back, then she and Tyler headed off toward the stairs.

They were in the stairwell when they heard a loud bang, and then the entire building shook. Tyler grabbed Shenin and pulled her into the corner of the stairwell, shielding her with her body. They heard secondary explosions.

"What the fuck!" Tyler yelled as the building shuddered with every loud explosion.

When the lights dimmed, Shenin pulled out her phone and activated the flashlight application on it.

"Let's get out of this stairwell," Shenin said. "Head up—I want to see if we can get onto the third floor."

Tyler took Shenin's hand and led her up the stairs. Putting her hand on it to make sure it wasn't hot first, she tried the door from the stairwell. She had to put her shoulder against it to force it open. Smoke and debris were everywhere.

"Kash! Baz! Kit!" Tyler shouted, not hearing any reply. "What the fuck happened?" Tyler said as she and Shenin carefully picked their way around ceiling tiles and large pieces of plaster that had been knocked off the walls. "Try the radio," Tyler told Shenin. "See if you can get ahold of Gage."

Shenin tried the radio but couldn't get anything but static. "Whatever it was probably took out the radio antenna on the roof."

"Damn it," Tyler said as they moved in the direction of the executive offices. "Careful, babe," she said when they encountered wires hanging down.

They moved further into the debris, then they got to Kashena's office.

"Kash!" Shenin yelled, while Tyler worked at clearing debris. There was no answer.

"Okay, help me with this," Tyler said, gesturing to the bookcase that had fallen halfway across the doorway. "Careful..."

When they'd moved the bookcase they could see Kashena lying on the floor. Her head was bleeding.

"Kash!" Shenin edged around a pile of debris to kneel next to Kashena. "Kash! Can you hear me?" She touched Kashena's face and felt her neck for a pulse. "She's alive, she's just out," Shenin said, checking Kashena over. "Looks like she smacked her head. "Kash! Hey! Come on, wake up! Ty, go see if you can get to Baz."

"Okay," Tyler said, going to the next office where Sebastian was usually located. She saw him—he was pinned by the bookcase that had fallen in his office. "Shen! I need you!"

"I'm coming!" Shenin called back, moving to the doorway.

Gage was just coming up on the OES offices when she saw the two helicopters collide, right over the building.

"Fuck!" Gage yelled, pushing the stick forward to get closer.

"Easy," Jocelyn warned. "We don't want to get caught in an explosion here."

"Kit's in there, Gun—we have to get in there!"

"Okay, easy. Just set it down here, and we'll go in."

"Fuck, fuck, fuck..." Gage chanted as she set the helicopter down at the outermost edge of the mostly deserted parking lot. Before the rotors had even slowed, Gage was unbuckling her harness and moving to the door.

"Whoa, slow down. Wait for me," Jocelyn said.

Gage waited, practically bouncing on the balls of her feet. Jocelyn got up; they got out of the helicopter and made their way to one of the stairwells that looked undamaged. It took both of them to yank the door open—it was wedged shut due to the impact of the crash. Gage took the stairs two at a time, her mind racing, trying to figure out where the helicopters had hit compared to where their offices were. As they reached the third floor, Gage ran headlong down the corridor.

"Jesus, Jock! Check the fucking doors. If there's a fire you're gonna kill us both!" Jocelyn shouted, running behind Gage.

Gage slapped her hand on the next door, and then yanked it open, giving Jocelyn a pointed look. Jocelyn simply grinned unapologetically in response.

They made it executive offices area and were shocked by the damage.

"Kit!" Gage yelled, trying to get to her office.

"Gage!" Tyler yelled back, hearing her voice but unable to see her.

"Ty?" Gage queried. "Where's Kit? Have you seen her?

"No, we're trying to unpin Sebastian. Is Gun with you?"

"Yeah," Gage called back. "But we're going to need to get through some shit to get over there. Where the hell is Kit?"

"Gage, help me with this," Jocelyn said, her hands on a large piece of ceiling tile.

Gage rushed to help; inside of five minutes they'd cleared a path to Gage's office and then to Sebastian's next door. Jocelyn went to help Tyler and Shenin, while Gage entered her office.

"Kit!" Gage yelled, trying to look around. She moved toward her desk, and that's when she saw Kit lying on the floor behind her desk. "Shit!" she shouted, climbing over her desk to get to Kit. She shifted her chair out of the way and saw that Kit was bleeding at her head, and there was a piece of ceiling tile on her. "Gun! Get in here!"

Jocelyn appeared at Gage's door almost instantly.

"Did you clear Baz?" Gage asked.

"Yeah, he's unconscious," Jocelyn said, climbing over Gage's desk like Gage had moments before. "But he's not pinned anymore… Oh Jesus…" she uttered as she saw Kit bleeding. "Okay, let's move this." She put her hands to the ceiling tile, feeling a piece of metal slice into her hand but ignoring it as Gage grabbed the other side. "Carefully, up and away, Jock…"

Gage nodded, then lifted. The ceiling tile was heavy, and it took all their strength to move it, but finally they heaved it away from Kit's body. Gage was on the floor immediately, touching Kit's face and checking for a pulse.

"Okay, her pulse is strong," Gage said, relieved. She checked Kit's neck and didn't feel any damage there. "We need to get her out of here. I really don't want to move her, but we don't know if this building is going to come down, and it's likely on fire considering all the smoke I'm starting to see." She stood. "I'll get her. Can you shove any of that out of the way? I don't want to try carrying her over this desk." She gestured to the debris to the side of her desk.

Jocelyn tried to shift the debris but wasn't able to budge it in the slightest.

"Ty, Shenin!" Jocelyn yelled.

Both women appeared immediately and went to help Jocelyn, seeing that Gage was holding Kit. Within minutes they had the area clear, and Gage was able to carry Kit out to the corridor and lay her down. Kit was coming to at that point.

"Babe, I need you to stay right here, okay?" Gage told her.

Kit nodded, looking like she was still out of it a bit.

Gage and Jocelyn went back inside to help with Kashena and Sebastian.

Kimber had made it down to the second floor, noting smoke was starting to fill the air. She walked into the corridor that led to Harley's office. When she got there she saw that much of the damage to the building was on that side. The ceiling was caved in at one end, far too close to where Harley's office was located.

"Oh God," Kimber breathed. "Harley! Shiloh!" she yelled, moving toward the area, careful to avoid hanging wires that were sparking.

As she got closer, she could see a helicopter blade through the opening in the ceiling. There was a clear liquid dripping from the blade, and she smelled fuel.

"Harley!" Kimber called again, knowing things were very dangerous.

"Kimber?" Shiloh called from inside Harley's office. "Kimber!"

Kimber moved to the office door and saw Shiloh on the floor, holding Harley's head in her lap.

"She won't wake up and I can't find her pulse, but my hands are shaking... Please find her pulse..." Shiloh said, crying.

Kimber had to swallow a couple of times and steady her hand. She kneeled next to Harley and touched her neck. She took a couple of slow deep breaths to calm herself, then pressed lightly.

"She has a pulse!" Kimber cried happily. "But we need to get out of here. Fuel is leaking from that helicopter, and the wires over there are sparking. We need to go, Shiloh," she said authoritatively as she stood up. "Help me get her up. We're going to have to carry her."

"Okay," Shiloh said, so overwhelmed with relief that Harley was alive that she could barely breathe. Standing, she helped Kimber pick

Harley up. Fortunately, although Harley was tall, she didn't weigh much.

Kimber took Harley's legs, and she and Shiloh headed toward the stairs.

"Careful of those wires!" Kimber said, shifting to get around them.

When they got to the stairs, they went down them carefully and got out of the building.

"Look, there's the helicopter!" Kimber said. "Gage and Gun must be here. Let's take her over there; they're going to want to get her to medical right away."

Shiloh nodded as they moved toward the helicopter.

Kashena had come to and was there to help them with Sebastian. They couldn't get him to wake up for a long time, so they started to move him. Shenin, Tyler, Gage and Jocelyn had managed to carefully wrestle his unconscious body onto the emergency evacuation stretcher from the stairwell. They were worried about back injury, since he'd been pinned at waist level and at a very bad angle. They'd gotten him all the way to the corridor, then had to set him down—he was solid muscle and a fairly big guy at six foot three and two hundred and twenty pounds. Sebastian stirred then, groaning loudly.

"Baz, lie still," Kashena told him. "We're worried about your back, but we've gotta get out of this building."

Sebastian was breathing heavily and seemed to be in severe pain.

"We got you," Gage told him. "Just relax, okay?"

Kashena carried Kit in her arms; Gage hadn't wanted Kashena trying to carry Sebastian because of her head injury and possible unknown injuries. Kit was light, so it was easier for Kashena to carry her.

It was the longest trip any of them had ever done, and they'd all been on twenty-mile humps in the military with the heaviest pack imaginable. By the time they managed to get him down three flights of stairs, they were all sweating and panting madly.

As they got outside, they saw Kimber and Shiloh standing near the helicopter, with Harley lying on the ground.

"Jesus," Jocelyn growled. "Fuckin' Army," she muttered as they carried Sebastian to the helicopter.

"Is Harley okay?" Gage asked as they got to the helicopter.

"She's got a strong pulse, but she hasn't regained consciousness," Kimber said.

"Okay, let's get them both into the copter. We'll take them over to the Los Alamitos Medical Center." Jocelyn picked Harley up and handed her to Tyler, who'd already climbed into the Firehawk. "Was there anyone else left in the building?" Jocelyn asked Kimber.

"No," Shenin said. "We let everyone else go."

"Good, thank you," Gage said, thinking this could have been so much worse.

Within an hour, Harley had been assessed and had come to. She had a head injury, but not bad or life threatening. Sebastian was in worse shape—a couple of discs had been damaged in his back and he was temporarily paralyzed, but the doctors assured him and a completely freaked-out Ashley that it would ease as the swelling in the discs subsided.

It was later discovered that, as Gage and Jocelyn had seen, two Army helicopters were set on the same flight path. The air traffic controller had gotten confused with so much traffic. With all the smoke in the air, the pilots hadn't seen each other until it was too late to avoid the collision. Fortunately they'd both made it out alive.

***

The week before Christmas, the small town of Fort Bragg was besieged by lesbians. The first wave included Jocelyn, Sable, Gage, Kit, Tyler, Shenin, Harley, Shiloh, Sydney and Mia; they were joined by Ashley and Sebastian as well. They had flown up a week ahead of time to do some celebrating of their own. Sable had chartered a plane and Gage had flown them. The rest of the group who would be attending the wedding were flying up on Christmas Eve in BJ Sparks' plane.

They checked into the Beach Glass Inn, having rented the entire inn for themselves as well as having rented rooms in another local hotel, the Beachcomber Inn, for the night before and after the wedding.

They arrived just before a nasty storm. It poured down rain, and the wind whipped the trees and created a pounding surf that punished the coastline. The proprietor of the inn happily chatted with them and told them some of the history of the area.

"So Glass Beach is really the original location of the city dump," the woman said. Her name was Maggie.

"And that's the glass that's there?" Sydney asked, enthralled by the story.

"Yep! It's been smoothed out by the ocean," Maggie said, her gray eyes twinkling as she smiled.

"We have got to check that out!" Sydney said to the group at large.

"Well, hopefully it'll be a nicer day tomorrow," Maggie said. "You should try to take the Skunk Train too—it's a great way to learn about the area and its history with lumber." She looked at Sable and Jocelyn.

"So you two are getting married at the McCallum house in Mendo?" she asked, smiling brightly.

"Yes," Sable said, smiling back.

"Aww, beautiful place, that. It's too bad you couldn't get married on the bluffs, but I guess that would be a summer-wedding thing. My daughter got married out there on those bluffs," Maggie gestured toward the bluffs, her face taking on a sad look. "She lost her wife a year ago though, cancer, nasty thing." She shook her head.

Jocelyn and Sable glanced at each other, understanding exactly what she meant. Later, they had dinner by the fire and listened to the wind howl outside. After dinner, everyone retired to their rooms.

"I've made a decision about something," Sable said to Jocelyn as she sat in front of her in the claw-foot tub with bubbles all around them.

"And what's that?" Jocelyn asked, sliding her hands over Sable's arms, holding her close, her lips against Sable's temple.

Sable turned around, staying within the circle of Jocelyn's arms but looking up at her seriously.

"I want to take your name," she said.

Jocelyn stared at her, surprised to the point of being unable to reply. Then she shook her head. "Your agent is going to kill you, babe. You've always been known as Sable Sands…"

"And now I want to be known as your wife."

The last incident, when Jocelyn had run into a burning building to rescue their people, had solidified her resolve to be completely committed to Jocelyn, privately and very publicly.

Jocelyn looked at her for a moment. "It's up to you, babe, but you don't have to do this to prove anything to me."

"I want to be Sable Mann, okay?" Sable said.

"Ma'am, yes ma'am," Jocelyn said, grinning. "But you're going to have to protect me from your agent and publicist."

"Hey, they work for me, not the other way around."

Jocelyn smiled. "Uh-huh."

"Are you sure it's going to be okay for you to take a month off?" Sable asked then.

"Yes, I'm sure," Jocelyn said. "Gage owes me for making this move back to San Francisco. Are you sure you're okay with doing that?"

Gage had decided that it would be better to place themselves more strategically in the state; she'd become concerned that with so many things happening in Southern California, they didn't have proper executive decision-making powers in Northern California. She'd asked Midnight for a special dispensation to make Jocelyn a co-director and have her run a San Francisco satellite office. Midnight had been exceedingly happy with the way OES had handled the multiple fires throughout California and had happily approved the dispensation.

Jocelyn was taking Sydney for IT and quite possibly Kimber for logistics, since there was no way Gage would give up Shenin. She was still working on her other positions. The agreement was that as long as Jocelyn could take a month off for her honeymoon with Sable, she'd do it. Gage had happily agreed.

"I'm happy being wherever you are, Jocelyn," Sable said, smiling warmly. "I've already got Zaiden looking for houses there."

Jocelyn shook her head. "Jesus, I don't even want to know how much something is going to cost in San Francisco."

"Just don't ask. It'll be safer that way," Sable said, winking at Jocelyn.

Jocelyn rolled her eyes. "At least I'll be making better money as a director, but I can guarantee it wouldn't pay for a house in San Francisco."

"You'd be surprised," Sable said, "but it doesn't matter. Just don't let your butch brain stew on it too much."

"My butch brain, huh?"

It had become their private joke, since Sable had once made a very public comment about never dating butches because if she'd wanted to date men, she'd date Jake, her bodyguard.

"Mm-hmm." Sable put her back to Jocelyn's chest again and slid her hands down Jocelyn's legs under the warm water.

"Mmm... What's going on there?" Jocelyn murmured as Sable's hands slid up her inner thighs.

"Well, we need to entertain ourselves..." Sable said, her voice trailing off as she touched Jocelyn, making her moan.

Jocelyn moved her lips to Sable's neck. "Yes, yes we do..."

In another room, Gage, Kit and Caitlyn were having a lively discussion about the properties of wind and how it couldn't actually bring the ocean into the inn. Regardless, two hours later, Caitlyn was firmly in bed next to Gage. Gage had Kit on her left shoulder and Caitlyn on her right. She smiled at her two girls. Kit and Gage had gotten married a month before. It had been a small ceremony, with Kit's family in attendance, and of course the group, as well as some of the people from OES. Kit hadn't wanted to make a big deal about it, since she had already been married. She'd asked Gage if it mattered to her; Gage's response was that she'd happily run off to Vegas and elope to avoid a huge wedding.

Gage was asleep when she felt a tiny hand on her face.

"Mama?"

Gage looked down at Caitlyn. "Mama's asleep, honey. What do you need?" she asked softly.

"No." Caitlyn shook her head, putting her small hand on Gage's cheek again. "You mama," she said, smiling brightly.

"Ohhh," Gage said, feeling her heart skip a beat at the sweet endearment from a five-year-old. "What is it, baby girl?"

"I'm thirsty."

"Okay, let's see what we can do about that without waking Mom up, okay?" Gage whispered.

Moving as carefully as she could, she was able to keep from waking Kit. Gage grabbed her sweat jacket off the chair and picked up Caitlyn's robe, holding it out for Caitlyn to slide into.

"Let's go see what we can find," Gage said, smiling.

Caitlyn nodded, looking excited by their adventure as she reached up to take Gage's hand in her little one. The two of them made their way downstairs and into the kitchen.

"Oh, score!" Gage said as she found chocolate chip cookies and milk.

"Yay!" Caitlyn said, clapping her hands.

Kit found Gage and Caitlyn sitting in the kitchen, eating cookies, drinking milk and blowing bubbles in the milk to see who could get their bubbles higher. Standing in the doorway, Kit smiled. She couldn't believe how lucky she'd gotten. Not only was Gage the most amazing person Kit had ever met, but she was amazing as a mother too. Caitlyn had taken to Gage instantly, and she rarely took to strangers, but Gage had been different right from the beginning. Watching them, Kit still couldn't believe that Gage was actually her wife. Her life was so dramatically different than what it had been a year and a half before. That was all due to Gage McGinnis.

"Hi, Mom," Gage said, seeing Kit standing in the doorway. "We're having a late-night snack."

"I see that," Kit said, walking over to stand next to Gage, kissing her on the lips and looking over at her daughter. "So who's winning?" she asked, gesturing to the bubbles in the glasses.

"So far, she's got me on the ropes," Gage said, winking at Caitlyn, who grinned happily.

"Well, I think I need to get in on this." Kit grabbed a glass and poured herself some milk.

The three of them stayed up for the next hour, having a grand time.

***

Shiloh stirred, turning over to see that Harley was already awake.

"Did you even sleep?" Shiloh levered herself up on her elbows.

Harley looked down at her, her blue eyes catching the sunlight coming through the windows.

"Some," Harley said, gazing around the room. "Strange place, weird noises, strange sheets..." she explained offhandedly.

Shiloh suppressed a grin; she knew it was Harley's ADHD talking.

"Coffee?" Shiloh asked.

"Please," Harley replied, smiling brightly.

"Want to walk over to that local shop?" Shiloh asked. "It looks beautiful out there."

"Yeah," Harley said. "Okay if I text Syd, or is this a me-and-you thing?"

"Yes, text Syd." Shiloh appreciated that Harley had asked; she'd been so much more focused on their relationship since the incident with John Garcia.

A half an hour later, Harley, Shiloh, Sydney and Mia walked down the street toward the Headlands Coffee House. The four made an interesting group.

Harley was dressed in her usual jeans and black Harley-Davidson boots; today she wore a black hoodie with a rainbow barcode and the words "Born This Way" on it, and a jean jacket with black leather sleeves. Her white-blond hair was pulled up in a ponytail, exposing the brightly colored rainbow under-dye that reached three inches past her shoulders.

Sydney wore black skinny jeans tucked into black combat-style boots, with a blue hoodie that said "Pro·gram·mer n. An organism that turns caffeine and pizza into software" in white letters. Over that she wore a black leather motorcycle jacket, looking very butch.

Then there was Mia with her pastel rainbow hair, wearing jeans, tennis shoes, and a pink sweater with Sydney's jean jacket over it. Shiloh was the only regular-looking one, albeit beautiful with her chestnut-brown hair with blond highlights and her moss-green eyes, complemented by the dark-blue sweater she wore with jeans, knee-high black leather boots and Harley's black-and-blue Harley-Davidson jacket.

When they walked into the coffee shop, every head in the place turned. There were a number of smiles and nods, and Shiloh breathed a sigh of relief. It seemed that Fort Bragg didn't have any problem with gays. They ordered their coffees and grabbed a table to sit and drink them at. At one point a woman walked in; she had short dark hair and a very definite butch look to her. She was wearing dark-blue BDU pants, a shirt with a Cal Fire patch on the upper arm, and black combat boots. A lot of people greeted her, and she smiled and waved or nodded to everyone. Her eyes touched on their group, and she smiled, inclining her head to them as she made her way to the counter.

"Morning, Mandy," the woman said to the girl behind the counter.

"Hey, Hunter, your usual?"

"You got it," Hunter replied, smiling.

"Looks like it's going to be a nice day," Mandy said, smiling shyly at Hunter.

Sydney saw it and raised an eyebrow. "Think the whole town is gay?" she whispered to Mia, making her giggle.

"We could hope," Mia replied.

"Yeah, that storm beat the crap out of the cliffs though," Hunter said in answer to Mandy's comment. "Gonna be some serious clean-up out there."

Mandy nodded. "We had some flooding in the backroom too. That wind was murder."

"Tell me about it," Hunter said. "It blew a few of Heather's trees over. Don't know if I'm going to be able to save them."

Mandy grimaced. "That sucks."

"She'd say it was nature," Hunter said with a slight grin.

Mandy passed Hunter her coffee, and Hunter handed her a few bills. "Keep the change," she told Mandy with a wink.

"Thanks, Hunter. You be safe out there."

Hunter turned around, nodded to the group again, then walked out.

Harley looked at Sydney. "Nice to see our own kind here."

"Yep," Sydney agreed.

Back at the hotel, Sebastian woke to the feel of his wife's hands on his chest, her body over his.

"Well, good morning," he said, smiling up at her.

"Good morning." Ashely kissed his chest softly.

"I see you're planning on taking advantage of the lack of child…" Sebastian's voice trailed off as she moved down his body, kissing as she went. "Jesus, Ash…" he moaned as she continued lower.

Sebastian was grateful that things had finally started working again in that department. He'd been ready to throw himself off the nearest roof when a certain crucial body part had refused to do its job when needed after the accident at the building. Whereas the paralysis in his legs had gone away in a matter of three weeks, it had taken a lot longer elsewhere. For a normally extremely virile man like Sebastian, that was pretty much a death sentence.

Ashley had, as usual, been extremely patient and had assured him that things would be fine. In the end she'd been right, but it had taken far too long, and Sebastian had been becoming desperate. He prided himself on being able to satisfy his wife quite sufficiently—he was competing against the specter of Jet Mathews, lesbian sex god extraordinaire from what Sebastian had heard. Ashley had been involved with Jet before she'd met him. He'd had very definite inferiority issues with that at first. It had been rough, since Jet and Sebastian were also good friends, but Sebastian had been jealous in a way he'd never been before. It had been out of what had proven to be love for Ashley, the only woman to ever fully capture his heart and hold on to it firmly.

They made love, both of them exclaiming loudly in their release. Afterwards, Sebastian heard his phone ping. He picked it up and read the text message, laughing out loud.

"What?" Ashley asked, smiling.

Sebastian turned the phone to her so she could read it.

KASH: *Glad to hear everything is working properly again, but you're grossing out the lesbians. Keep it down, Ranger! LOL!*

Ashley laughed.

"I hope you're not going to let her get away with that," Ashley said.

"Hell no," Sebastian said, smirking as he tapped out a response.

BAZ: *Whatsamatter, Marine, can't keep up?*

They heard Kashena's laughter in the next room. Sebastian got a response a moment later.

KASH: *Any day, Ranger, and twice on Sunday.*

In the next room, Kashena put her phone back on the nightstand, turning to pull her wife back into her arms.

"You two…" Sierra said, shaking her head.

Kashena simply chuckled.

"So what do we do?" Sierra asked Kashena, continuing the conversation they'd been having before Sebastian and Ashley's antics had shaken the walls.

"Honestly?" Kashena said. "I think I should have Baz talk to him."

"Seriously?" Sierra asked, her eyes widening.

Shortly before their trip, Sierra had been putting clothes in Colby's room and had accidentally knocked over a box on his nightstand. Condoms had fallen out. Sierra had panicked and gone straight to Kashena about it.

"I think he'd take anything that was said better from Baz, Sierra, I really do."

"Yes, but what is he likely to say?"

"Let's talk to him," Kashena said.

Later that morning they did just that.

Sebastian looked surprised by the request but nodded, agreeing with Kashena that Colby would likely be a lot less embarrassed hearing things from a man than from either of his mothers.

"What would you say?" Sierra asked.

They were sitting out on the porch of the inn. Sierra sat next to Kashena on the loveseat-style chair, with a blanket and Kashena's arms around her. Sebastian sat next to Ashley, holding her hand and smoking.

"Well, I'd make sure he knows how serious having sex is in a relationship," Sebastian said. "It's not something to be messed with if you're not ready for the consequences."

Sierra nodded, liking what Sebastian was saying.

"I'd also tell him that he'd damned well better treat any girl he's in a relationship with with respect or his mothers will likely kill him," he added with a grin.

"Oo-rah," Kashena said.

"Are you having withdrawals?" Tyler asked Shenin, who had a faraway look on her face.

Shenin smiled. "I'm sorry, yeah. I kind of miss him."

Tyler grinned. "Yeah, me too," she admitted.

"We're hopeless," Shenin said, laughing.

Tyler winked at her wife. "Maybe we can Skype with Jenny later so we can get a fix."

Shenin laughed softly, shaking her head.

They were in the sitting room of the house, drinking coffee and just enjoying the quiet morning. They both looked up as Sable walked by them on her phone. She was arguing with someone about flower arrangements. She rolled her eyes at Tyler and Shenin and pointed to the phone. Tyler and Shenin laughed. Sable walked out the front door of the inn, still arguing with the person.

***

That day, the group went to Glass Beach, walking around and enjoying the beautiful coastline. The next day was spent shopping in Fort Bragg and Mendocino. On the third day, Sydney finally got her wish to get on the Skunk Train. Later they all had lunch at a local pizza place called Piaci Pub and Pizzeria. They again ran into Hunter, who was dressed this time in street clothes. Once again, many of the people in the pub greeted her. She smiled at everyone and noted the large group occupying the long trestle table near the door, inclining her head to them.

"Family," Sebastian commented to Ashley.

"For sure," Ashley said, grinning.

"She works for Cal Fire," Harley told Gage, who was sitting next to her.

"How do you know?" Gage asked.

"We saw her that first day at the coffee place. She was wearing a Cal Fire uniform. There's an office right down the street from our hotel."

Gage nodded. "She must live around here if she's around when she's not working."

"Just liking the family angle," Harley said, grinning.

Gage laughed, catching Hunter's eye when she glanced over at the sound. Gage inclined her head to Hunter; Hunter winked at her then turned back to the woman at the bar. She left a little while later with a pizza box in hand, smiling to the group as she did.

Later that day, they made their way to Mendocino, which was a few miles down Highway 1. Sable had rented three Escalades for the trip down. Jake drove one of them, Gage another, and Sebastian the third. There was a spirited race down the highway, ending in a tie between Gage and Jake. Sebastian was a close second.

There was a run-through of the wedding at the McCallum house. It involved only Jocelyn, Gage, Jake and Sable—Gage was acting as Jocelyn's best woman, as Jocelyn had for Gage the month before. Jake was giving Sable away. "Considering he's the only man I respect most days," Sable had told Jocelyn with a smile.

After the quick rehearsal, they all had lunch at Patterson's Pub and then walked around the bluffs above the ocean. Sable and Jocelyn were walking along, talking about where they should have dinner that night. Sable got a call; it was the florist again. Rolling her eyes, she picked up the call, holding her finger up to Jocelyn, who only grinned.

Gage and Kit were talking about the strange huge links of chain that stuck out of the ground in one area on the bluffs. Gage saw that Sable was on the phone, so she motioned Jocelyn over to involve her in the discussion. A heated debate ensued over what the chain could have been used for.

"It looks like there was some kind of dock," Gage observed, pointing to the wooden remnants farther out on the bluffs.

"Maybe," Jocelyn said, looking thoughtful. She glanced over to where Sable was gesticulating wildly at the person on the phone. She shook her head, then looked back down at the chain in the ground. "Something heavy, that's for sure."

"But the ocean is so far down," Kit put in. "How would ships have been way up here?"

"Tall ships?" Gage suggested.

Jocelyn glanced over at where Sable was talking to the florist, but she was gone.

"What the…" Jocelyn said.

"What?" Gage asked, even as Jocelyn started to run toward where Sable had been moments before.

As Jocelyn skidded to a halt, she looked around and then down, and her heart all but stopped. Sable lay twenty feet below on a rock formation—the cliffside had given way.

"Sable!" Jocelyn yelled. Sable didn't move. "Fuck! Gage!"

Gage was already running toward Jocelyn, turning her head. "Call 911, Kit, now!"

Kit was pulling out her phone as Jake got to them; he'd been up by the road securing the vehicles, figuring Sable was safe out on the bluffs.

"We gotta get down there," Jocelyn said to Jake. He nodded, starting to look for a way down. The cliff face was sheer; there was nothing to hold on to. Jocelyn ran to the right, searching for a way down, as Jake ran the other way doing the same.

Gage ran after Jocelyn, worried that she'd try something dangerous to get to Sable and get herself killed. "Kit, try to get Sable to respond to you! Gun, wait!"

"Help's coming!" Kit shouted to anyone who was listening.

"What happened?' Sydney asked as she and Harley came running up.

"Sable fell," Kit said, gesturing down at where Sable lay.

"Holy shit!" Sydney said. "What can we do?"

"Go grab Sebastian. He and Ashely were going into that toy store on the main street," Kit said, thinking that they might need sheer strength.

Tyler and Shenin got there then too, seeing what was going on.

"Shen, go flag down the emergency crew. I'm going to go see if I can get ahold of some rope or something," Tyler said, assessing the situation quickly.

"Good," Shenin said, turning to run toward the main road. Tyler did the same, heading toward the ranger's station to the right.

"Sable!" Kit called. "Sable, can you hear me?"

"I can't get down there!" Jocelyn yelled, sounding absolutely frantic. "Goddamn it! I can't get to her! Jake! Anything?"

Jake shook his head, holding out his arms helplessly.

Five minutes later, Jocelyn tried to literally climb down the cliffs to get to Sable, causing Gage to grab her and yank her back up with Sebastian's help.

"I can get down there!" Jocelyn yelled at Gage.

"Not without killing yourself! And how the fuck are you going to get back up?" Gage shouted. "Help is coming!"

"Where the fuck are they?" Jocelyn roared, her voice tinged with pure panic. Sable hadn't responded to any of their yelling.

As if in response to Jocelyn's query, they heard the sound of rotor blades cutting through the air. The helicopter was black with a gold stripe; it had no insignia on it other than its tail number. It landed a number of yards from the edge of the bluffs. Jocelyn ran toward it, stopping under the still-spinning blades. Opening the passenger door, she looked across at the pilot. It was the woman from the pizzeria.

"Get in. I'll get you down there," Hunter said, gesturing to Jocelyn.

Jocelyn didn't hesitate—she climbed inside and closed the door, as Hunter lifted off. Jocelyn picked up the other helmet and put it on.

"Use that harness there. You ever rappel from a helicopter?" Hunter asked.

"Fly them, yes; leave them, no," Jocelyn replied as she pulled on the harness. "But there's a first time for everything."

Hunter nodded, grinning.

"You need to get her off the rocks. The tide comes in fast this time of day."

Jocelyn nodded, feeling a bit sick suddenly.

"You with me here?" Hunter asked, seeing Jocelyn close her eyes and swallow convulsively.

"We're getting married in two days," Jocelyn told her.

Hunter smiled. "Then get down there and get your girl."

Jocelyn gritted her teeth and steeled herself. Hunter cleared the bluffs and lowered the helicopter, her rotor blades mere inches from the edge of the bluffs.

"Squeeze to slow down. When you're ready, just speak into the mic and I'll lift you both up to the clearing I landed in. I see the ambulance coming now. Go!"

Jocelyn opened the door and, without hesitation, rappelled down to where Sable lay. She felt the rope loosen and knew that Hunter was feeding her slack so she could get to Sable.

"Sable!" Jocelyn kneeled down next to her. She touched Sable's cheek and thought she'd pass out with relief when Sable's eyes fluttered open instantly.

"Jocelyn?" Sable said, seeing the helicopter hovering above them and then feeling the splash of ice-cold water near her. "What happened?" she exclaimed, starting to get up.

"Hold on, babe, don't move yet." Jocelyn did a quick assessment and felt confident that Sable hadn't broken anything major in the fall. "Okay, I need to pick you up, babe. Put your arms around my neck… Son of a bitch!" Jocelyn exclaimed as cold water dowsed her from behind. "Fuck, that's cold!" She heard Hunter's chuckle in the headset.

"Warned ya," Hunter said, a grin in her voice.

"Okay, babe, let's go. Put your arms around my neck... Good, now hold on tight, okay? I won't let you go, I promise. Just hold on to me." Jocelyn stood up with Sable in her arms. Sable buried her face in Jocelyn's neck.

"Okay, we're good. Let's go before I get another bath," Jocelyn said into the headset.

The next thing she knew, she and Sable were being lifted off the ground as the helicopter ascended. It was a quick swing over to the landing area. Jocelyn released the harness as her feet touched the ground. The paramedics took Sable out of her arms then, but Jocelyn followed them to the ambulance, even as she turned and saluted Hunter, who nodded, giving her a thumbs-up as she landed the helicopter.

Gage and the rest of the group ran up to the helicopter as Hunter turned off her engines, waving to the rangers who were coming toward her.

"Well, that was handy," Gage said, extending her hand to Hunter. "I'm Gage."

"Hunter," the other woman replied.

"Yours?" Gage asked, gesturing to the helicopter.

"Yep."

"Nice..." Gage said, grinning. "Is this a Euro?"

"You fly?" Hunter asked in surprise.

"Anything I can get my hands on. Apaches in the Army."

Hunter smiled. "BlackHawks."

Gage nodded. "So, whatcha doing on Christmas night?"

"Uh..." Hunter stammered, looking confused.

"I'm betting you're getting a wedding invitation now," Gage told her with a wink.

"Well, I guess I'll be going to a wedding then," Hunter said, grinning.

Jocelyn was extremely relieved to hear that Sable was, for the most part, unharmed from her fall. She'd bruised up her side and right hip but was otherwise okay.

"You scared the shit out of me!" Jocelyn told Sable when she was finally able to see her.

"I'm sorry," Sable said, grimacing. "One second I was standing there talking to that infernal florist—who I fired, by the way—and the next you're standing over me with a helicopter hovering above our heads."

Jocelyn chuckled, shaking her head, reaching out to touch Sable's face.

"Fired the florist huh?" she said.

"Yeah," Sable said. "Less of that flowery stuff now."

"I'm all for that."

"Of course you are!" Sable said, smiling all the same.

"They're working on getting you out of here," Gage told them as she walked into the room. "And this is the pilot that saved your asses." Gage gestured to Hunter, who stood in the doorway.

Jocelyn strode over to Hunter, extending her hand.

"Thank you," she said. "I can't begin to tell you how much you saved our asses just now. Jocelyn Mann."

"Hunter Briggs," Hunter responded. "This winter has really given our cliffs a beating. That last storm was just the kicker. I've told the rangers that they need to rope off those cliffs, but the city council is fighting it." She canted her head at Sable. "But since Sable Sands just about bought it on those cliffs, I'm guessing the threat of a fairly expensive lawsuit might do the trick."

222

Jocelyn saw the mischievous sparkle in Hunter's silver-gray eyes. She looked over at Sable.

"What do ya say, babe? You feeling litigious?"

Sable grinned. "I believe I may be," she said. "I'll call my lawyer and have him make contact with the city council today."

Hunter smiled widely. "You'd be doing a great public service."

Sable and Jocelyn both grinned, knowing that Hunter was trying to do what was best for the public at large and not worried about profit margins.

"So, how were we lucky enough to gain your assistance today?" Jocelyn asked Hunter.

"I tend to monitor the radio calls during my off time. Lots of time on my hands these days," Hunter said, her expression slightly shadowed at that last statement.

"And you just happen to own a helicopter?" Sable asked.

"When you live way up here, you tend to need fast transportation," Hunter said. "I just happened to be running her up when I heard the 911 call. I knew that the tide was coming in, and I wasn't sure they'd respond with a copter, since the call wasn't transferred to Cal Fire. So, I came down."

"Well, we certainly owe you," Jocelyn said.

"I asked Hunter what she was doing on Christmas night..." Gage put in.

"Oh, well, you definitely need to come to the wedding if you're free," Jocelyn said, glancing over at Sable, who nodded vehemently.

"I'd be honored," Hunter said.

"Perfect!" Jocelyn said, smiling brightly.

***

The wedding of Sable Sands to Jocelyn Mann went off without a hitch, aside from a distinct lack of flowers. Gage toasted them and wished them a happy life together, as did many of their friends. Jocelyn, resplendent in a perfectly cut tuxedo, also gave a toast.

"To all our friends, who gave up their Christmas night to be with us tonight," Jocelyn said, smiling. "I personally want to thank all of you for your support and love during this incredibly rough time in my life. Most of all, though," she said, turning to Sable, her face serious, "I want to thank my bride. Sable, without you I never would have made it through the last year. As some of you may not know, my mother died of ovarian cancer a few years ago." She paused, letting that sink in, and she saw a number of heads come up at that information. "As such," she continued, gazing down at Sable, who was watching her with a reserved look on her face, "when I was originally diagnosed, I had no intention of doing treatment. I wanted to go out my way, not cancer's way." Her voice shook as she looked over at Gage, whose eyes filled with tears instantly. "It was Sable who came back, at Gage's request, and showed me that I did have something to live for and that fighting might be a possibility. As you can see," she said, gesturing around them, "it worked. So, to Sable, for saving my sorry ass, and I just hope I can make it worthwhile her going through hell with me and coming out the other side. Cheers."

Everyone raised their glasses. "Cheers!"

The end of the *WeHo* series

You can find more information about the author and other books in the *WeHo* series here:

www.sherrylhancock.com

www.facebook.com/SherrylDHancock

www.vulpine-press.com/we-ho

Also by Sherryl D. Hancock:

The *MidKnight Blue* series. Dive into the world of Midnight Chevalier and as we follow her transformation from gang leader to cop from the very beginning.

www.vulpine-press.com/midknight-blue-series

The *Wild Irish Silence* series. Escape into the world of BJ Sparks and discover how he went from the small-town boy to the world-famous rock star.

www.vulpine-press.com/wild-irish-silence-series